Gods, Ghosts, and Kahuna on Kauai

Gods, Ghosts, and Kahuna on Kauai

A John Tana Novel

Bill Fernandez

Design, Sketches, and Photographs by Judith Fernandez
This is a work of fiction and the product of the author's imagination except for these characters: Hawaiian royalty: Dowager Queen Emma, Queen Kaahumanu, King Liholiho, King David Kalakaua, and Princess Liliuokalani; also, Molokai leper colony priest, Father Damien. Some of the events involving them are based on actual events but the conversations are fictional. Any similarities to persons living or dead are purely coincidental.

Published by Makani Kai Media 2017
Library of Congress Number: 2017915163
ISBN: 0999032658
ISBN 9780999032657
Makani Kai Media, Kapaa, HI

www.kauaibillfernandez.com fcb: Bill Fernandez Hawaiian Author
A Kauai Made Approved Product

Dedication

I lovingly dedicate this book to

my wife,

Judith Fernandez

Acknowledgments

The Hawaiian ethic of family, ohana, means no one accomplishes alone. We are who we are today because of those who came before us and who are with us along our path of life. I particularly want to say mahalo (thank you) to my teachers, especially those at Kamehameha Schools, who turned this barefoot boy into a serious student. Vernon Trimble, my sophomore class advisor, stands out in my memories as a strong influence on me, urging me to attend college.

My editor and friend, Bill Bernhardt, taught me about commas and tries to mold me into a good writer.

Many others have helped me in many ways, encouraging me to continue writing. Thanks to the Kauai Historical Society, Kauai Museum, and Kauai libraries for honoring me by including my books in their publication sales and collections, and inviting me to give book talks. Bill Buley of *The Garden Island Newspaper* and his wife Marianne encourage me in many ways. Several people who enjoyed *John Tana, An Adventure Novel of Old Hawaii,* urged me to continue the story about my Hawaiian hero, John Tana, as he struggles to adapt to the take-over of Hawaii by Western business interests and religion. My neighbor Phil O'Rourke, particularly, urged me to continue. Cynthia and Ed Justus of Hanapepe Bookstore give invaluable advice, carry my books, and invite me to do book signings.

Without the encouragement, support, and hard work of editing, design, photography and sketches, publication, and promotion of my writings and book talks by my loving and devoted wife, Judith, I could not have written my books. All the credit for what I have written goes to her.

Reviews of Bill Fernandez's Books

Review of novel *John Tana, an Adventure Novel of Old Hawaii:*

"The author expertly moves the plot along (through short chapters), and the **vivid** and intriguing details of **Hawaiian daily life in the 19th century ring true**...For the setting and era alone **ripping adventure yarn**...Fernandez,...a **native Hawaiian**, is an **authentic voice** for John and the Pacific archipelago's turbulent history. **Plot twists** come thick and fast...[an] undercurrent of John's **love for Leinani**..."

Kirkus Reviews, Jan. 6, 2017, (Emphasis added)

—~—

Review of novel *Cult of Ku*:

"Fernandez...incorporates Hawaiian history, folklore, and labor struggles into a **1920-set mystery packed with violence and**

murder...he offers many **fascinating insights** into the era...An edifying novel that **explores cultural conflicts in Hawaii** between the world wars..."

Kirkus Reviews, Jan. 2, 2016, (Emphasis added)

—w—

Reviews of memoir *Hawaii in War and Peace:*

"A **riveting** account of his experience of a world in disarray both during and after the [**second**] **world war**...But what makes the **grandest impression is the personal** side of the narrative."

Kirkus Reviews (Emphasis added)

—w—

Len Edwards, Los Altos, CA: "One of the best **coming-of-age** books I have ever read."

Prologue

Gods, Ghosts, and Kahunas on Kauai is the second novel in a trilogy which began with *John Tana, An Adventure Novel of Old Hawaii.* The series opens when native Hawaiian orphan John Tana loses his inherited farm to a sugar planter in 1867, and concludes with the third novel at the time of the overthrow of the Hawaiian Kingdom by the Western business interests in 1893. In those turbulent decades of the clash of cultures, the indigenous, communal-living Hawaiians and their nation were swept aside by Western commercial interests and religion which still impact Hawaiians.

The first novel, *John Tana*, begins in 1867 when the seventeen-year-old native Hawaiian orphan loses his inherited farmland (*kuleana*) on Maui to a sugar baron, Robert Grant. Unbeknownst to John, Western business interests had begun to seize control of communal lands for sugar planting. He sails his outrigger canoe to Lahaina, Maui, seeking distant family, and encounters whaling ships and sailors who torment him. He finds his Aunt Malia and two cousins: David, a young man succumbing to liquor and women, and Leinani, a beautiful young fourteen-year-old. John learns that liquor and a Christian-forbidden romance can lead to trouble. He befriends Ah Sam, a Chinese former plantation worker who opened a business which competes with established stores. John interrupts an attempted shanghai and rescues kidnapped Leinani. When he learns the sugar baron hired a killer (Gonzales) to find him, John escapes with his family and Ah Sam's family, sailing his canoe to the island of Oahu.

John finds life on Oahu and in the new city of Honolulu more complicated. He works in the taro fields and Ah Sam opens a restaurant. But David continues his risky life in bars where he meets new friends who attack the family. Leinani is sent to a private girl's school for safety and John joins a secret martial arts (*lua*) group in the mountains. A future king (Kalakaua) invites him to join the militia. When a Chinese man is accused of killing his white employer, the city erupts into racial violence. John finds him a Hawaiian lawyer (Joshua). Leinani introduces him to Maria, a French classmate who falls in love with John. After Leinani's true ancestry is revealed in a confrontation with Robert Grant, James Kingsley, and Aunt Malia, John realizes his love for her is not forbidden. But before he can act, she is persuaded to marry rich, white, James Kingsley. John is bereft, but realizes Aunt Malia is right: "A Hawaiian man has nothing to offer a woman but poverty, while a rich white man can give her and a future family a comfortable life."

When John learns he will be arrested for an alleged rape of Maria and that the killer Gonzales has found him, he escapes to the island of Kauai hoping to find a peaceful life. Leinani remains in Honolulu.

This volume of the trilogy, *Gods, Ghosts and Kahuna on Kauai,* begins as John sails to the island of Kauai. The sugar industry is expanding, taking control of land and water. John finds work as a plantation security guard and returns to farming while family resistance to Christianity creates conflicts. Mysterious things happen: an octopus attacks someone, a shark saves another, a boar hunt and an owl might be omens of death. The tropical lushness of the island creates a mysterious world.

The third novel of the *John Tana* historical trilogy will complete the story of how the West eventually defeats the Kingdom of Hawaii and overthrows the monarchy as the century comes to a close. Expected publishing date is 2018.

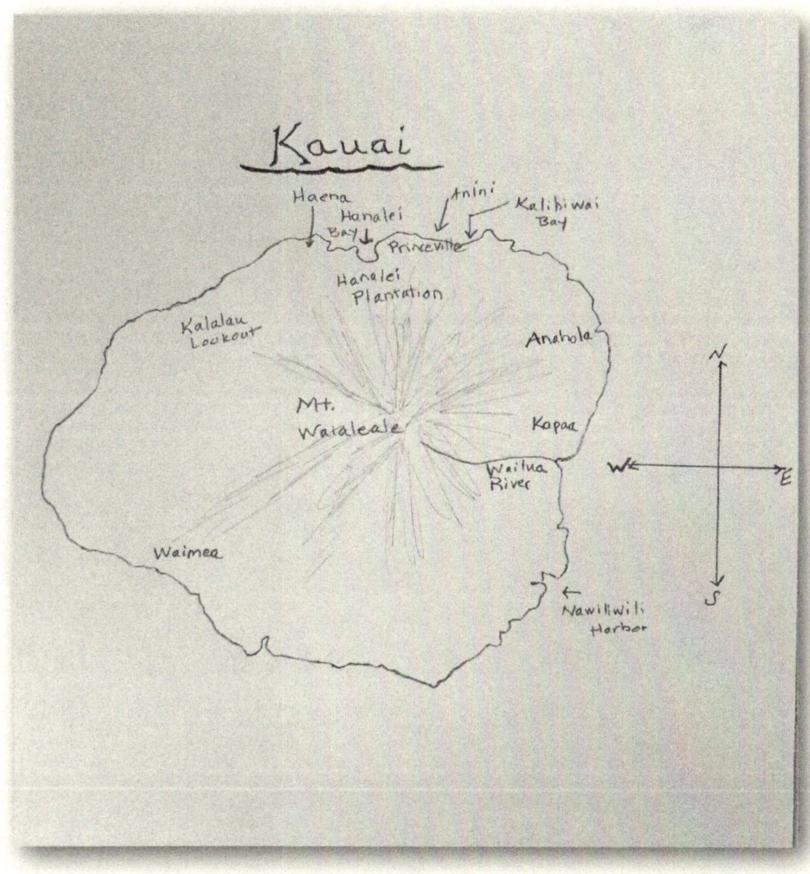

Kauai

Other Works by Bill Fernandez

Non-Fiction Memoirs

Rainbows Over Kapaa

Kauai Kids in Peace and WW Two

Hawaii in War and Peace

Fiction

Grant Kingsley Series:

Cult of Ku, A Hawaiian Murder Mystery

Crime and Punishment in Hawaii

John Tana Series:

John Tana, An Adventure Novel of Old Hawaii

Chapter 1

With the wind dying, John Tana watched his double-hulled canoe lumber over low waves that rushed toward shore. A thin crescent moon shone through a haze of low-lying cumulus clouds dark with rain. John felt a sense of deep depression that he knew comes before the arrival of a violent storm. His wooden boat with members of the Alapai family lay off the Waianae coast a few miles from Kaena point on Oahu. A young girl, Mahealani, lay asleep on a platform between canoes, oblivious to the deluge rushing toward them.

"It's sixty miles of open water to Nawiliwili Bay," Moana, the elder son of Haku Alapai, said.

"I know the danger," John answered. "Seventy-five years ago, Kamehameha's invasion fleet bound for Kauai was destroyed by a storm near this coast. Thousands of dead warriors covered the beaches."

"Pull into shore. Ride out the winds on land."

"Last time I landed at Waianae, we barely got away before the women of our party were raped."

John studied the coastline looking for lights. He saw none and wondered if this part of the forbidding coast might be uninhabited and safe.

Thunder echoed through the heavens with a giant clap making the sail post shudder. Sheets of rain smashed into the ocean flinging up fountains of sea water. Beyond the dark horizon pulsing light flashed across the sky then died as explosive thunder sounds followed. The once placid sea began to roll in waves of foam.

"Steer for shore! Wait out the storm!" Moana begged.

John shifted the angle of his paddle, moving the vessel toward land he could not see. The moon no longer shone through the heavy clouds. Flashes lit the coast for brief moments. With its sudden light, John glimpsed a grim coastline with waves smashing into huge boulders.

"Rocks ahead," Moana yelled.

Through heavy rain, John saw masses of white foam swirling around a bleak stone-covered shoreline. There was no sand. Yet he could feel the gentler ebb and flow of waves washing up and back from a safe shore. He aimed the vessel where his instincts told him he would find a place to land.

"Pull hard on the left side, on the right, back off," John ordered.

The double canoe lifted on a wave shoving the boat toward a looming wall. Mahealani screamed.

The canoe turned broadside to the dark stone. If his senses were wrong, John knew they would be hurled into the boulders. "Paddle hard," he yelled as he switched his stroking from one side of the craft to the other, guided by the push-pull of the waves. With its seven passengers and all that John possessed, the double canoe plunged into the darkness as the crashing sea and thunder roared in his ears.

Lightning flashed across the horizon, a gleam of yellow reflecting from its light. John steered toward the sand. A monster swell smashed into the rocks flinging the sea high above the canoe filling it with water making it sluggish to maneuver. John knew another giant comber would doom them. "Pull hard on the right."

Into the eddy between waves the vessel moved at a slow pace. The starboard outrigger scraped rocks. The grinding of wood on stone brought chills of despair to John's heart. *Who would die if they overturned? How many would be bashed onto the rocks?* For a moment, he thought they should have stayed in the open sea, but Moana was right, they had to make land or all would perish in the storm.

Despite pain, John mustered his strength, forcing the canoe into the darkness toward the fleeting glimpse of sand that a lightning bolt had revealed. The double canoe lumbered forward, awash with water.

A wave lifted them, sped the craft onward, but the overweight canoe did not plane on its crest. Instead, it wallowed back into its trough. Another comber struck. Water cascaded over the vessel until it was full. John knew he could not maneuver the craft so he kept it pointed to the spot of yellow his senses told him must be ahead.

A surge of the sea pushed the canoe. John heard the crunch of sand rubbing against the twin prows of his boat. "Out!" Onto the beach he tumbled followed by the rest of the *ohana.* A wave swung the vessel sideways. "Grab an edge and hold it while I bail."

"Good landing job," Moana said.

Within moments the water in the dual hulls was emptied and the canoe pushed higher onto the shore. John, Moana, and his cousin Eleu set up a lean-to for the women, Mahealani, her mother Anuhai Alapai, and two sisters. Despite protests, John knew that the real danger on the Waianae coast is not the sea, but men. He insisted on a watch being mounted and took the first shift.

Rain pelted him causing shivers to wrack his body. His thoughts wandered to a time years ago when a Waianae thug lusted for Leinani and moved to take her. He shoved the man away, assuming a fighting stance. His friend Kawika intervened.

He looked to where Mahealani slept. Her infatuation pleased him. It made up for the loss of the woman who meant everything to him.

Moana relieved John and he hunkered down between the rocks finding a comfortable place to rest. His back hurt, his head and side ached. He dozed, the pelting rain making it difficult to sleep. The storm ended before dawn. He fell into an uneasy slumber. Weak sunlight filtered through low clouds hurrying over the island. Bare feet tramping on stone forced John awake.

Chapter 2

Robert Grant watched the storm blow past Nuuanu and onto the mountains of Waianae. Rain which deluged the valley during the night moderated to a drizzle. At the breakfast table, he studied his daughter. Leinani held her hands folded in her lap, her eyes cast down as if fascinated by the elegant scrolling of the silver service set before her. From an exquisite porcelain pot a maid poured tea into delicate demitasse cups.

"It is settled then. You will marry James Kingsley," Grant said, casting a look of triumph toward his wife. The sun that had been obscured by the heavy rain clouds flashed over the ridgeline, lighting the alcove where the Grant family took their breakfast.

From her place in a wicker chair, Leinani avoided the stare of her father. She kept her eyes lowered, fidgeting with the dainty French half-cup ringed with a rim of gold. "The kitchen didn't strain this tea before it was served," she answered.

"Nonsense, the staff knows their duties. There is nothing wrong with the tea," Sheila Grant said, her voice cold and disapproving. Then she moderated her tone, "James Kingsley is quite handsome and very rich. We would welcome him into this household."

"Don't push the issue. A marriage is not a simple thing. You know that when a choice is finally made it is forever. Leinani has given me her word that she has accepted Kingsley's offer. That is true, isn't it?" Grant asked, drumming his fingers.

Leinani raised her face, a small tear trickled from an eye. "Yes," she whispered.

"Good, then all we need to do is settle on a date. Sheila will plan the wedding. It will be the finest ever in Honolulu. Malia may come, but we will not invite the other Makananis."

"Why not?" Leinani interjected suddenly, thinking of John.

"They are not family. I'm investigating your blood line. You may be related to King Kamehameha. It is not proven yet, but likely. I do not wish your royalty to be tarnished by those who are not."

"My dear young lady," Sheila added, her tone sarcastic. "We must make suitable explanations for you and Robert's unfortunate affair. Kingsley knows your story and brushes it aside, but others will gossip. We will make your past intriguing, majestic, and dripping with kings and queens."

Grant gave his wife a quizzical look. "You sound very dramatic. Don't make the tale such a fairy story that none will believe it."

"Trust me, Robert, I will keep it modest, but I do not want shame to be visited upon this wedding. It must be without blemish, like Leinani's white wedding gown."

"Since we are all agreed on what will be done, it is time for school. I will have a manservant escort you to Saint Sebastian. Sheila, come to the den where we may talk."

In the coolness of his opulent smoking room, Robert Grant motioned his wife to a comfortable red leather chair and sat opposite her. He paused for several moments considering what to say, then on an impulse stood and began pacing the room.

"Robert, whatever is the matter?"

"That kid who has bedeviled us is somewhere at large in Honolulu."

"What are you saying?"

"You recall the young Hawaiian who came to our door looking for my daughter. He even went to her school to find her. I tried to get rid of him, but failed."

"I don't understand. Did you attempt to kill him?"

"You know I would not do anything of the sort. But one of my employees thinking to ingratiate himself with me took it into his head to eliminate the boy."

"And he failed to do so. Why is that a problem for you?"

"The employee is dead. He was found at the base of Diamond Head."

"So, he was hiking and had a fall."

"A rifle lay on the rim of the crater near where he fell. My gun, it had been fired."

Sheila paused for some moments, her eyes flickering over the design of the rug in the room. When she spoke, her words were terse. "Your man shot the boy. He fought him. He fell. The boy is alive and will make a complaint."

"That sums up the problem. An inquiry before the wedding is embarrassing enough. Worse would be an accusation from this *kanaka,* especially if he appears at the ceremony."

"I see why you did not want the Makanani family at the event. We must think of what to do. Are there any reliable men in your employ?"

"Only the one who died."

"There must be others who can assist us. I will talk to our house boy. You check with your employees in Wailuku. Do you have a picture?"

"From the newspaper."

"That will do. You're close to the sheriff, start a rumor that this child may be a person of interest in the death of your man. Maybe offer a reward. Once he is found we will permanently stop him from interfering."

Astonished by his wife's vehemence, Grant stopped his pacing. He looked at her in a new light. He knew she hated Hawaiians, barely tolerating Leinani because of Kingsley and the money he could provide the family by the marriage. "You are willing to eliminate this boy?"

"If the choice is preserving our wealth or the life of this Hawaiian then for me preservation is paramount."

Chapter 3

John heard feet scrambling over stone. He rose. Above him, the sky showed patches of blue, foretelling good weather to come. To his left, mounds of rock bent upward to the forbidding profile of Kaena Point. Behind him curved a small sand bay ending in stone that stretched into the sea.

He loosened the sling at his waist and retrieved three round pebbles from a pouch. Moana, who had taken the last duty shift, lay asleep. Above him, descending on boulders that ringed the cove came three big men in loincloths wielding clubs.

"Get up," John said, nudging Moana with his foot.

"Let me sleep."

"Up, there are people coming to take our women."

"What?"

"Waianae guys intend to cook us for breakfast and save the girls for dinner. Wake up the others fast."

Moana scrambled up and headed to the women's hut. John raised his hand. "Ho, halt. We are here in peace."

The three intruders stopped their rush. One of them said, "You on our beach."

"I'm sorry we did not get permission to land," John said, his tone humble. Then he added, "You saw the storm last night, we needed shelter." As he said this his feet sought a firm purchase in the sand. He clutched the finger loop of the sling cord in his middle finger and the wrapped knot of the second cord between the thumb and forefinger of the same hand. In his left he grasped three almond-shaped stones. The sling's leather pouch swung slowly above the beach.

Mahealani awakened with a squeal. Her younger sisters arose and cast frightened glances at the strangers, then huddled against a side of their lean-to.

"You on our land. Those women belong to us," one of the men said, pointing.

"We apologize. The big winds forced us to land. You may not have our women," John answered, inserting a stone into his sling.

"Huh! If you no give women. What you give?"

"Nothing."

"What! We goin' bust your ass."

John's arm whirled. A stone struck the head of a Waianae man. He grimaced, reached to his temple, and collapsed to the rocks. A second man stumbled down the boulders, his club raised.

With his left hand aiming at the on-rushing enemy, John dropped a stone into the sling's pouch, whirled, and flung it into the man's groin. The attacker gasped and fell to his knees. His club dropped from his hand, bounced twice, then came to rest between boulders.

The sling cords swung around, and John released a third stone into the pouch but did not throw it. The uninjured man stopped and backed away. He stretched out his clenched fist.

"We'll be back, with help," he yelled as his cronies crawled after him.

Mahealani came to John. "Why didn't you talk to them?"

"Waianae men don't talk. They kill the men and rape the women."

"How do you know this?"

"I've been here. What they want is you. When they end their fun, they make you a slave or a sacrifice. Either way, you're finished forever."

"I can't believe they could be so evil."

"Let's not wait to find out if I am wrong. Everybody leave!"

John inspected his canoe for damage. Outside of a scraped outrigger, the vessel was seaworthy. "Eleu, Moana, help push this to the sea."

The three men carried the boat into the water. It rose and fell with the waves. Mahealani ran to help the three women in the shelter. They were slow to abandon their hut.

John searched upland, worried that the delay would give time for the enemy to regroup. "Hurry!" he said, impatient with them. On the boulders above, he saw movement.

"Eleu, hold onto the canoe. Moana, help the women in." John rushed to retrieve the club wedged in the boulders. Men scurried down the rocks like a horde of black crabs. Frightened, the women scrambled into the canoe.

"Everybody paddle."

"What about you?" Mahealani screamed.

"Go!"

Fear drove the ohana to force the canoe into the sea. A dozen yards from shore, a despondent Mahealani leaped over the side.

John swung his club into the body of the closest pursuer, and then flung it into the mass of men coming behind him. He turned and sprinted across the sand and dove into the water.

When he surfaced, the young girl was at his side. "Why?"

"To help you."

"Swim."

The couple stroked for the canoe that slowly moved out to sea. Rocks peppered the water. Several men leaped into the ocean. Mahealani proved to be a powerful swimmer and gained the side of the canoe before John. She hesitated.

"Get in," he said, pulling himself into the vessel. He seized a paddle and pushed it into the water. Mahealani dangled in the ocean.

A Waianae man tried to grasp her. John hit him. Another seized an outrigger. Moana speared him with a gaff. Blood colored the water. The pursuers backed away. The ohana forced their paddles into the sea. Rocks flew from the shore, some smashing into the canoe, none hitting flesh.

John surveyed the angry men on the beach, their fists held high. "Whether we want to or not I guess we are heading for Kauai."

"I still think you should have talked to them," Mahealani complained.

"Oh, is that why you leaped over the side? To talk to them?"
"No, to save you," she answered, tears coming into her eyes.
"Sorry." John folded her into his arms and kissed the tiny drops away.

Chapter 4

Kauai, 1874

Early in the morning of the third day after leaving Waikiki, an exhausted John Tana and the Alapai ohana paddled into Nawiliwili Bay, Kauai. They used the strong ocean swells to surf onto Kalapaki Beach. A rushing stream emptied dirt into the ocean where they landed. Several men were casting hand lines into the murky water. John called to one of them. "What are you catching?"

"Moi."

"The king of fish. Can we camp here?"

"Sure, beach belongs to everyone, but the parson or the sheriff might visit with you folks. Don't get people paddling in from the sea much. Usually they come on the *Kilauea*." The fisherman spat into the water. "And that's not often. Danged ship is always running onto a reef or breaking down."

John thanked the man and returned to the ohana already asleep on the sand. He smiled when he saw that Mahealani had spread out a kapa and was waiting for him. They made eye contact and she motioned him to her. Pulling John onto the cloth, she wrapped it around them, melding her body into his.

"Time to sleep."

Mahealani did not answer. Her eyes had closed. Her breath fanned warm over his chest. The heat of her body excited him, but he controlled his arousal, too tired to complicate his life once again. His head nodded onto her hair and he fell into a deep dreamless sleep.

"Wake up. Fornication is illegal," a harsh voice said, followed by a stick prodding his back. John stirred, but did not rise, exhausted by the effort to cross the unruly Kauai channel.

"Get up or I'll bash your head in." The stick prodded harder.

John unrolled from the blanket. Blazing light from the setting sun over Haupu ridge dazzled him for a moment. Mahealani lay asleep, though one hand groped where he had been. He stretched his arms relieving the ache of paddling. He flexed his fingers and yawned. A lean Hawaiian, full-bearded, muscular, with a broad-brimmed black hat stood a few feet from him, a long baton in his hand. As he suppressed another yawn, John asked, "What do you want?"

"You married to her?" the man asked, pointing his stick at the sleeping girl.

"No. What's it to you?" John demanded, irritated by the man's surliness. He was thirsty, hungry, in pain, and in no mood to be confronted by a local. The rest of the ohana still slept so he decided to deal with this belligerent man alone.

"Don't sass me. Is she married to someone else? Are you?"

"None of your business. Leave us alone," John said, his fists clenched at his side as he assumed a fighting stance.

"Don't get huffy. I'm Deputy Sheriff Mailoa and I enforce the law of the Lord God Jehovah. He says that adultery must be punished and unmarried sex is an abomination. Answer me. Are you two married to someone else?"

John suppressed his anger. He knew he was in trouble in Honolulu. He did not want to add to his woes by an incident on Kauai. "Sorry. I didn't know who you were. No, we are not married to others."

"That's better. Since I can't charge you with adultery, which is a very serious offense, all you're guilty of is fornication. I'll have to take you both to the judge. He will skin you. Toss the two of you in jail. Of course, if I get something to forget the whole thing—"

"You will let them go," a gaunt person in a dark woolen suit interrupted.

Mailoa turned toward the man sitting on a fretting mare. He flinched. "Reverend, I'm just enforcing the law. This couple, they were fornicating on the beach."

Mahealani was awake, rubbing her eyes, her sackcloth garment belted tight around her waist. The minister looked at her, then John, and said, "Mailoa, you must be mistaken. They're both fully clothed. Young lady, were you having sex with that man?"

"No," Mahealani stammered.

"You," the Reverend pointed at John. "Were you having sex with this child?"

"No," John answered, mystified by the accusation made by Mailoa and grateful that he could give a truthful answer.

"See? There is nothing to charge them with. Be off and let me speak with them."

Mailoa left grumbling, and the parson slipped from the saddle. The rest of the ohana stirred. Sunlight blazed golden over the ridge as the day ended. "Reverend Saul Will," the man said, extending his hand. "What are you folks doing here?"

"We're coming from Honolulu to make a new home on this island," John answered, not wanting to admit that he might be a runaway outlaw. He thought the minister stared at him and he dropped his eyes, worried that they might reveal the guilt he felt for the events of the past several weeks. He knew he had not raped Maria. He knew that he fought Shaw and his men to save Ah Sam. It was Gonzalez who intended to kill him. But he also knew that missionary law could be like sticky rice. He might be caught in a web of circumstances and found to be a criminal.

"Are you Christians?"

"I've been baptized. I can't speak for the rest of the family."

"So, you're not related to the others in your group." The reverend pointed at Mahealani. "Are you Christian?"

She shook her head then blurted, "My family not Christian."

"Then you are heathen. You have not accepted God as your savior. You will never enter the heavenly kingdom prepared by the Lord since the foundation of the world. Jesus when he comes in clouds of glory will judge you evil and banish you to hell. Do you practice the outlawed dark arts?"

Mahealani hung her head, her hands rubbing along her sides. Her feet fidgeted in the sand.

"Reverend," John interceded, "these are good people. I have not been with them long, but I have never seen them practice the old religion. Maybe you can show them the way to God."

Will cast a baleful eye on John. "A capital idea. Gather your people and follow me."

"We must wait for the rest of the family coming from Honolulu."

"Good, more sinners to save. When you are reunited bring all to the mission. Any local will direct you there. If the sheriff bothers you again tell him that you are under my protection. The law man arrests newcomers for no reason at all, just so he and that scallywag judge can split the criminal fines. Members of my flock alert me when strangers come so I can save them from the corruption." The Reverend tipped his hat, mounted his horse, and left.

Chapter 5

For three months the Alapai family lived at the mission house learning God's word and providing useful services to the ministry. John attended the church school to educate himself, for the Reverend had said, "The law of this nation is based on His book and the spirit of His words. To own private property, you must be of good moral character and know the words of the Lord Jehovah." John did not know the truth of this claim, but he realized that something written, that could not be changed, was better than the old system where you obeyed the whims of the ruling chief.

Mahealani wanted to bed with John and Haku Alapai approved. But Reverend Will refused to permit a quick marriage saying, "She must learn Christianity and drive paganism from her soul for God says that marriage is forever. You people move in and out of relationships without caring. This makes marriage just a cloak for lechery. I will not permit a wedding until Mahealani is Christian and I am satisfied that the marriage will be permanent."

Governor Paul Kane visited the mission and befriended the ohana. He urged them to go north. "You will find land available there. Many Hawaiians have died, leaving fields vacant. The Chinese have taken over Hanalei Valley. They are planting rice where taro used to grow. See my agent on the north shore, Al Akaka, he will help you find land."

Before the family left, Mahealani accepted Christianity and wanted to marry John.

Reverend Will objected. "You are too young. In another year, I might reconsider."

John was happy with this decision. He needed time to heal. He went with the Alapai family to the north shore and met Akaka who directed them to a flat plot of ground at Wainini Beach. He assured them that the owner,

Princeville Plantation, would permit them to farm there since they considered the land unusable for sugar cane.

The group acquired a lease from Princeville, built homes, pens, and enclosed ground for growing taro. They settled into a peaceful existence at a place known by Hawaiians as "the gentle waters."

Chapter 6

Honolulu, 1874

Robert Grant slammed his hand on the ornate mahogany bar of the Downtown Club, grabbed his Scotch and strode to the second-floor window of the private conference room. He stared at the street below. Honolulu had changed since he was a child; then it was a squalid port city with pitted pathways and grass shacks. The Hawaiians he knew were lazy, interested only in liquor and fornication, unable to make a living or build something worthwhile. Today the city was different, wide rock-paved streets, sidewalks, public conveyances, modern buildings, law and order, all because of sugar money. "Damn it," Grant said. He swigged his drink, the smooth warmth of the Scotch calming him.

"What ails you, Robert?" Bruce Jones asked, a distinguished man with salt and pepper hair, long sideburns that narrowed to a cleft chin, and an aristocratic nose.

"We have problems gentlemen. Ever since the Arctic freeze destroyed the fleet the whaling business has dried up. Add to it, the Southern States are producing sugar, lots of sugar, and the U.S. Congress has slapped huge tariffs on imports from Hawaii." Grant ceased his staring and walked over to a sidebar fumbling in a box of cigars.

"Didn't you make a ton of money during the Civil War?" Paul Smith asked.

Lighting the tobacco, Grant inhaled until the tightly rolled weed burned red, then he spewed a stream of smoke into the room. "Yes, but the war ended nine years ago. Today, the sugar beet competition is fierce and import charges into America eliminate profits. We need to get our products into that country duty-free."

"I agree. Factoring has dried up. No one is building sugar mills," Jones said, and added, "Our Hawaiian government is doing nothing to help us."

"That worthless Lunalilo is dead. He was monarch for a year and achieved nothing," Smith agreed.

"It's time to take over." Grant waved his cigar, its ash sprinkling the red carpet overlaying the floor. "The United States gunship *Portsmouth* is in harbor. We could persuade Minister Pierce to land marines and seize power."

Jones shook his head. "Pierce favors American annexation of Hawaii, but he won't act without a direct order from Washington. And there are British and French warships in port. They might not like the U.S. taking Pearl River. It could mean war in the Pacific."

"Smith, how about your Honolulu Rifles, couldn't you get your men to act?" Grant asked.

The stubby shipping magnate shrugged. "We're just getting organized. Weapons and ammunition haven't arrived from California. We need at least a year of training. Remember, my boys are volunteers, they work during the day."

"Force is not the answer. The dead king did not name a successor. The House of Nobles picks the new ruler," Jones said.

"Hah, and we control the House," Grant answered, puffing his cigar and blowing a stream of smoke into the white-walled room. His elation cooled, and his brow furrowed as he asked, "Who are the likely candidates?"

"They have to be Hawaiian, and they must have some relationship to Kamehameha the Great," Jones said. "There are only two who could be considered, Dowager Queen Emma and David Kalakaua."

"Then our influence in the Nobles is meaningless," Smith said. "Emma wants Hawaii for the Hawaiians and will not let these islands draw closer to America. As for Kalakaua, he has opposed giving up control of any Hawaiian property, the quid pro quo needed to get a reciprocity treaty approved by Congress."

The private conference room fell silent. Grant walked over to the sidebar and retrieved a bottle of Scotch, bringing it and three glasses to a round, felt-covered table. He eased three chairs around it, and invited his two associates to join him as he poured alcohol and passed out fresh cigars. "What are you celebrating?" Jones asked, a puzzled expression on his face.

"I know Kalakaua, he can be bought."

"With the votes we control, he would be the next king, delightful," Jones said.

"And once he's elected we rush to Washington, offer up Pearl River, and get our treaty. No need for a revolution, or foreign intervention." Smith smiled, lit his cigar, blew a perfect smoke ring, and thrust a finger into its center. "Hah! Bull's-eye." He laughed, glancing at his companions.

"My advice gentlemen, is to acquire as much land as you can, especially along the streams and rivers. Mark my words, with reciprocity in place, scores of mills will spring up, and sugar profits will skyrocket," Grant said.

"We will need thousands of new workers, tons of supplies, all imported by my ships," Smith added, rubbing his hands. "And factoring business will boom."

The financier smiled. "Instead of bringing in more Chinese, we'll get some other foreigners, Portuguese, Germans, Spaniards, and Fijians, play one off against the other. That way we keep the hired help under control, no strikes."

"I agree. Too many pigs mean labor unrest. It's time to acquire more land, gentlemen. My son-in-law has been investing in a new sugar plantation starting up in Kilauea, Kauai."

"Isn't there already an existing mill in Hanalei? Princeville?"

"Yes. It would be our competition on the north shore, but Kingsley tells me the operation is close to bankruptcy. If it happens we can take advantage of that plantation's misfortune and control half of the sugar fields on the island. I'm heading to Wailuku to add to my holdings." Grant lifted his glass, sloshing the amber liquid around its rim. "Gentlemen, to profits."

Ten days later, from the same second floor window of the Downtown Club, Grant watched rioters being herded to prison by marines from the *U.S.S Portsmouth.* "Fools, they didn't realize that once Kalakaua was elected king he would ask for help from the foreign ships in port."

"It was touch-and-go once the vote was announced at the courthouse steps. Shooting started, fights began, a legislator was thrown out the window," Smith said.

"I barely escaped from the melee that followed. Kalakaua took my advice. He sought American and British aid. Their sailors responded quickly."

"What's next?"

"Once Emma's people are in jail, we send the new king and a delegation to Washington. We offer control over Pearl River for a reciprocity treaty."

"Will Congress accept the idea?"

"Yes. The United States doesn't want any other foreign power to seize the finest potential harbor in the Pacific and gain an advantage. We can make a deal."

"Won't the Hawaiians oppose loss of their land?"

"They have for a decade. But this time whatever the protests are we must have that treaty. As a guarantee against disorder, I'll make sure there is always an American ship in port with marines. We'll approach the transitional change slowly. At first the agreement will be that no foreign power may have the use of Pearl River. With time, our group will slowly give America full control of it. Smith, prepare to become a millionaire."

The two men left the second-floor drawing room and headed downstairs. "Are we going out on those riot-ridden streets alone?" Smith asked.

"No, I want you to meet someone I just hired."

A six-foot-three-inch giant rose from a chair near the front door. His long blond hair flowed around his ears and descended onto his shoulders. His face was clean-shaven and unmarked either from disease or brawls. His biceps were huge, bulging out like melons from his short-sleeved white blouse. His broad chest tapered to a narrow waist. His appearance was of a man of Herculean strength.

"Smith, this is Sven Larsen. Once he was a whaler. But that time is over. He needed a job and I hired him as my body guard."

"You're a big man. How heavy are you?"

"I maybe two-hundred-thirty pounds. I work in iron foundry. Lift weights every day for six years before I go to sea."

"How old are you?"

"I think maybe twenty-one going twenty-two. Mr. Grant, I bring friend like you ask. He need job too. Name is Gunter."

Another blond man rose from a chair. He was not large in size like Sven, but lean and well-muscled. His face was covered by a full beard. Blue eyes peered out from bushy eyebrows. His finely chiseled nose and thin lips gave him the aspect of a cultured gentleman.

"Very good, tonight we will see what you men can do. There's a bunch of Emma's malcontents outside spoiling for a fight and Smith and I need to get home. Let's go."

They left the building. The roadway was empty, but Grant heard shouts. "Hurry along. We can avoid trouble if we move fast." But when they rounded the corner onto Nuuanu Street, a group of Hawaiians faced six British marines holding rifles with fixed bayonets.

"There's that haole that voted for Kalakaua. Get him," someone in the unruly mob yelled. Stones were pitched and a segment of the belligerents charged Grant. Larsen swung a belaying pin into the lead man of the pack. He faltered. The Swede picked him up like an empty sack and hurled him into the others.

"Get them Gunter," Larsen yelled. The two former whalers tore into the Hawaiians with clubs flailing. The melee was soon over. Three men lay injured on the pavement and the rest of the cowed mob fled.

A sergeant of marines, looking sharp in red coat and blue pants, came to Grant and said, "Thank you for your assistance. I thought to retire my men rather than risk injury. Your two chaps saved the day. Right handy with clubs they are. We'll get these fellows off to prison." The sub-officer saluted, called his detachment to come to him, and took the beaten men away.

"You've got yourself a nice pair of body guards," Smith said, admiration in his voice.

"I agree. They acquitted themselves well tonight. They will make great guardians of my interests."

The four men headed for home. Grant felt happy for his good fortune in replacing his loss with younger men. "I'll give you two an assignment on

Maui. I need to keep some striking Chinese in line. You use a whip? Ride a horse?"

When the two nodded in the negative, Grant said, "You will learn. A horse and whip are essential to making these coolies obey. Once you have taken care of Maui, I may want you to find a *kanaka*."

Chapter 7

Wainini Beach, Kauai, 1874

John and Haku Alapai dug into soft soil next to a small forest. Water from a stream trickled into the berm-enclosed field where they worked. A small distance from them were houses and pens that the family had built between the sea and the trees.

"There is a dangerous *uhane* that haunts Wainini. You will need my protection," a voice whispered. The two men stopped their digging and stared at a shrunken, nut-brown Hawaiian standing on the dike they had just completed. Until he spoke he had been invisible.

"An uhane? A spirit enslaved by black magic. Ghosts like that exist only in the mind of the foolish. We are Christians and do not believe in the dark arts," John said, scowling at the creature who weaved from side to side as if drunk.

"I didn't accept Christianity," Haku protested. "I want to hear about this uhane that roams the area."

"Uhane?" Mahealani asked, walking up to the men, a gourd of water slung over her shoulder. She studied the ancient. His hair was scraggly white. A necklace encircled his throat with a graven image of a god resting on the ribs ridging the skin of his chest like a washing board. The man held a staff clutched in his hand, his fingernails long and black. "You are a *kahuna*," she said, awe in her voice.

"Yes," Haku agreed. "Are you *ana ana*?"

"We don't want to traffic with death dealers," John interrupted, watching the old man as his weaving stopped and he fastened his eyes onto Mahealani.

"You want something very much. Come to me."

As if in a trance, Mahealani stepped toward the creature. John leaped from the mud and held her back. "Leave her alone." The young girl struggled for a moment then went limp in his arms, breaking eye contact.

Light from the western sun struck the kahuna's eyes making them glow. He fixed a gallows stare onto Haku Alapai who averted his face to escape the satanic look. In a crackling voice the old man said, "The uhane comes in the night. It will enter your women for love or turn your men cold with the paralysis of death. If you make offerings of food and drink I will save you from him."

Haku croaked, "Where would we leave them?"

The kahuna's lips parted revealing teeth stained brown with *awa* juice, "By the dip in the ridge is an old altar. You may leave your offerings there." The old man looked at Mahealani, who had revived from her faint. She trembled, a hand fidgeted with her hair. Her feet treaded as if in a dance. "If you need me come to the altar. Bring gifts." A sudden breeze blew, raising clouds of dust. The kahuna moved into the small maelstrom and disappeared.

"Why did you agree to give him gifts?" John said, his voice harsh. "He's a slimy old eel trying to steal from us with his talk of evil spirits." He fixed his eyes on Haku and watched the sweat rolling down the older man's face, soaking his shirt. He wondered if the dripping was caused by heat, work, or fear. Mahealani's arms wrapped around his waist, her pretty face snuggled against his chest. John stroked her raven hair, rubbed his hand along her back. He felt her heart thumping and knew she was frightened.

"You're a Christian and say you don't believe in that stuff. But you once did," Haku said, his eyes wary, searching where the kahuna had disappeared. "I'm too old to change and Mama Alapai thinks like me. You take care of the Christian God for us and we'll take care of the old gods for you."

The breeze slowly died, and the sun burned orange-red over Makalena Mountain. Haku's eyes were cast down staring into the tilled field. "I didn't mention this, but my nephew has been sick for several days. He wakes up complaining that his feet are cold and the freezing is moving up to his stomach."

Mahealani gasped, pulling away from John, her eyes wild. "That is how the uhane comes. First cold feet, then legs, stomach, after that you die. Oh, we must go to the altar and give gifts."

John grasped her shoulders. "There is no such thing as ghosts. Why the boy is cold, I do not know, but it is not because of a cursed uhane."

Before the disagreement could turn into a raging fight, a voice called from the beach. "*Hui*, Alapai family, I need help." John glanced to the ocean and saw Al Akaka running across the field. When he came to Haku he said, "Some of Queen Emma's people are lost in the Alakai Swamp. I need men to help me find them."

"Where is that?" Haku asked.

"It's up there." Akaka pointed to a range of mountains. "If we go now, we can just make it to Wainiha by dark. Then start the trek up to the Alakai before dawn."

"Don't know those places, but you can have my son Moana, nephew Eleu, and John will help."

"Good. We must hurry. Whoever is up there will die if we don't find them."

Chapter 8

Mt. Waialeale

Before sunrise, four men ate a skimpy meal, broke camp, and began the trek along the Wainiha River heading for the Alakai near the summit of Waialeale Mountain. As they hiked, Akaka explained that the Dowager Queen Emma had come to Kauai on holiday after the election. Intrigued by the legends surrounding the ancient volcano and its huge swamp, she had secured a Hawaiian guide to lead a party of her courtiers, one hundred dancers, singers, and musicians. They had left from the southwest side of Kauai and walked to the opposite side of the dormant volcano near Wainiha Valley. The large group had spent the night on the heights overlooking the island. The next day they returned to Waimea and found that two of their party were missing. Expeditions were being mounted to find them. One came from the west, Waimea. They were the second, coming from the east side of the island.

"Damn, I'm sliding," swore Moana as his foot dislodged the edge of a thin trail sending a shower of rocks avalanching into the valley far below. John braced himself, tightening the rope looped around Moana's waist, pulling him back onto the skimpy, grass-covered trail.

Akaka, ahead of the men, stopped hiking. He called, "This is an old trail. Not used since some missionaries wanted to see the swamp twenty years ago. Poke your staffs ahead of you. Make sure the ground is solid. Don't depend on the guy in front. Each of you, watch where you place your feet."

John grimaced as he thought this was an impossible venture. The mountain they climbed was steep. Over the eons water had created deep fissures in the rock walls. In many places, it was a sheer drop. The heavy rainfall had made the ground slippery and treacherous. Above him the summit of Waialeale, crowned by trees and thin shrubs, seemed to wave in the wind. That will make it difficult, he thought, the heavy winds sweeping over the island could blow them over the edge and into the valley. He gave up his worrying to concentrate on the trail ahead.

Once at the top of their climb, Akaka passed out conch shells. "We will spread out. Blow every five minutes. Call after you trumpet: 'Melody, Hiram'. If you find them give two sharp blasts. I will stay here, clashing the cymbals from time to time. If they are found by one of you or the other search party I will clash my cymbals repeatedly. Mark your path so you can find your way back to me. Return by nightfall."

John plunged into the black mud of the swamp. To his surprise, the swamp was filled with color. Tall bushes studded with violets grew from the decaying earth. Brown, orange, even white, moss covered the trees and shrubs. But the entire aspect of the jungle was like being shoved into a primeval past before the creation of Adam and Eve. John blew his conch shell. He called the two names. He heard others trumpeting and occasionally the cymbals clashing. In the intervals, there was silence.

Hours passed. Mist swirled around him. A light rain made him miserable. John decided to return to Akaka. He blew his trumpet, called the names, then plunged into the knee-deep mud to return to base. A faint whimper came with the wind. For a moment, John thought it was branches rubbing in the breeze. But the sound came again, like the mewing of a sick cat. He shouted the names.

Silence.

He floundered through the muck. He sank to his knees in the morass. The swamp decay clung to his legs. He worried he had stepped into a sink hole that might pull him under. His feet searched for solid footing. He paddled with his hands, grasping onto anything hard. By pulling shrubs he moved through the muck until his feet felt solid ground. He heaved himself onto a berm overshadowed by trees and lined by low bushes. He followed a thin trail until it ended at a large depression of crumbled earth. He called, "Melody, Hiram". He waited. Mist and breezes swept up the valley, only a bird answered his call. He thought he had been mistaken by the sounds he had heard, but he called once more.

From below the precipice a weak voice said, "Help".

John peered over the edge and saw two people clinging to heavy brush. Their faces were gaunt. "Are you Hiram?" John called.

"Yes."

"I will drop you a rope. Place the loop around Melody and I will pull her up, and then you."

"I can't. I'm too weak."

"You must help. If I try to go down for you, we could all fall."

"I'm afraid," Hiram whimpered.

John found a tree, tied his rope to it, and rappelled to the stranded couple. Melody was feeble, incoherent, and could do nothing more than cling to the shrubs. When Hiram tried to grasp John, he pushed him away. "I'm taking Melody first. Then I'll come back for you." As he looped the rope around her and then himself, Hiram tried to seize him, begging, "Take me first." But he was too weak to do more than paw. Hand-over-hand John climbed to the summit. He found a safe place for Melody and told her that he would be back. He blew his conch shell twice and rappelled to Hiram.

When he reached him, the man blubbered. His hand flailed John's face. His sudden thrashing made the shrubs that held him crack and slowly bend downward. As Hiram slipped, he grasped John's neck, preventing the rope from looping around them. John seized the crazed man as the shrubs parted. He pulled Hiram to him, his feet wind-milling as they dangled over the abyss.

John held the rope in one hand while his feet searched for a purchase in the loam-filled ground of the cliffside. He prayed the tree he had chosen would prove strong enough to hold him and the frightened man. He tried to soothe him, but Hiram was beyond reason. His thrashing and the wet loam caused John's feet to slip over the moss-covered cliffside. The two men hung in the mist, thousands of feet above the valley floor.

Chapter 9

Honolulu

"Beautiful," Robert Grant said as he held out his hand to Leinani. She raised her face to his. Through the thin white veil, he admired her perfection. Her hazel eyes like his, and high cheekbones that gave her a glamorous look. A slender nose, full lips appearing almost wanton with the redness that had been painted on them. *With her light-colored skin and amber hair, she exuded an exotic beauty far different*, Grant thought, *from the dusky, blunt-nosed, and stringy-haired native women.* He rubbed his hands, delighted that James Kingsley would soon be wedded to Leinani. He would make good use of the wealth of this young financier, and knew he could become one of the most powerful men in Hawaii.

Grant drew the eighteen-year-old into him. He smelled her fragrance and for one of the few times in his life he felt affection. His father had been harsh and cruel. Grant realized now that his dad had driven kindness out of him and replaced it with a thirst for money.

"I promise I will always treat you with love and respect," he whispered as he walked her down the aisle toward Kingsley. He had assured him, "She is a virgin. You will be the only man to ever enjoy the fullness of her charms." He passed her off to the beaming rich man and assumed his seat by Sheila.

"You did a marvelous piece of work, she is radiant. How did you ever come up with that tale that she may be a granddaughter of our second king?"

His wife smiled. "I told you I would make her mysterious and rich with lineage."

"Do you, James Kingsley, take Leinani to be your lawfully wedded wife, to have and to hold from this day forward, for better or for worse, for richer, for poorer, in sickness or in health, to love and to cherish, from this day forward until death do you part?" the minister asked.

Grant smiled as he heard Kingsley answer with a firm yes. His lips turned into a frown when it came Leinani's turn, for he barely heard her answer. "She's still thinking of that Hawaiian scoundrel," he whispered to Sheila.

"Be satisfied. She said, 'Yes'."

Grant's smile returned. He had got what he wanted, financial salvation. He patted promissory notes wedged in his suit pocket. Kingsley had returned them earlier in the morning. Grant no longer faced bankruptcy. With his son-in-law's money, he would expand his operations.

"You have never liked my daughter," Grant said as he and Sheila walked to the reception in the parish hall.

His wife pursed her lips then answered, "Hawaiian women are trollops. I had thought she would be the same. You had her checked and satisfied James she was pure. Good enough for me, except I believed that pesky Hawaiian boy had his way with her."

"Thank God he fled and didn't show up at the wedding. I kept Leinani from reaching out to him by telling her there was a warrant for his arrest for raping a French girl. She believed me for she knew the young woman."

"Is there such a warrant?"

"Never issued, the girl and her father left for France which ended all claims."

"I have heard that the French girl's lover left for Kauai. Best check with your son-in-law where they will honeymoon."

At the reception Grant asked Kingsley about their plans for a vacation.

"Strange. Leinani wants to visit the north shore of Kauai. She claims that it is beautiful with broad white beaches and fabulous vistas. I have arranged with Princeville for them to use the old Wylie mansion. It overlooks Hanalei Valley. I'm told the view is spectacular and when the moon shimmers on the bay—"

"It can be very romantic."

But whom does she intend to be romantic with? Grant thought. *A scandal so soon after the wedding would ruin all my financial planning.*

As if an afterthought, Grant said, "I'm interested in Kilauea Sugar Company. It has just begun planting on Kauai. Will you speak with the manager? Evaluate the operation and form an opinion as to whether it would be a worthwhile investment."

"I'd be delighted to do so. Let's get the cake cut. I want to escape this party."

Grant grasped his coat sleeve before Kingsley pulled away. "I will be sending my man there, Sven Larsen. He will determine for me if there is ample water to support a first-class sugar operation. My servant may stop by to pay his respects and provide you with security."

"You think we may have trouble?"

"One never knows. I'm told the Hawaiians on the north shore are savages. It's best to keep them away from you. I know my man can protect you from scoundrels."

"Thanks for the offer. I'll keep what you say in mind," Kingsley answered, a worried frown on his face.

A half-hour later, Grant watched the couple leave in their phaeton, streamers attached to the rear axle fluttering in the wind. "That man is eager to bed her," Grant said to his wife. "It will be a torrid wedding night. He has waited more than a year while she finished school and reached her eighteenth birthday. He has displayed outstanding control, but I could see he was bursting with love for her."

"Yes, it is evident he is a man in high heat. But will that trollop meet his expectations?" Sheila asked sarcastically.

"I don't know. She certainly put off the marriage for as long as she could. What concerns me more is they are leaving for the north shore of Kauai."

"You investigated my hint that trouble might be brewing during the honeymoon."

"I don't know if it will. But I'm sending my man Larsen to watch them and make sure that John Tana does not interfere."

"And if he does?"

"Larsen will have orders to kill him."

Chapter 10

Kauai

"Stop fighting or we will both fall," John said, his tone angry. Hiram ended his struggles. John gripped the distraught man to his chest, his right hand holding tight to a loop in the rope. He prayed someone had heard his final call. He shouted. Their swinging increased, forcing him to stop.

He worried, they could not dangle forever. He knew if he let Hiram go he could save himself. That was not an option. They would make it together or die together.

He searched the moss-filled walls for a ledge or outcropping, but saw nothing except jagged stone. His feet brushed into soft grass slippery from rain. Hiram blubbered, "We are going to die." Tears slid down his face.

"Be cool, brah. I will need your help. I'm swinging right. Hang on."

John pushed off from the wet cliff wall, his feet searching for any purchase he could find. He remembered the days when he clung to a vine and swung over a pool as far out as he could go before releasing and plunging into the water. Today he found nothing he could land on. His arm ached, dangling with the weight of Hiram was taking a toll on his strength.

He spotted a flat area of the cliff wall. But he had reached the end of his swing and couldn't regain his sideways momentum. His back scraped stone as he fell back to his starting point. A new worry struck him, would the swinging rub the rope and make it part?

"Hiram, hang tight, I'm going to push off as hard I can."

He sprang to his right. He controlled his sideways momentum with his feet. He felt his toes touch something solid. With a prayer on his lips he pulled on the rope to reduce the slack. John's feet found flat ground. He felt tufts of grass. Will this ledge be firm enough? Could he release Hiram onto it? But he realized the man couldn't help. He clung to John like a suckling baby holds onto its mother.

He still had enough sideways momentum so he could pull himself and his burden onto solid ground. "Hiram, I'm going to set you down."

"No, no," the distraught man pleaded.

"I must. Place your hands inside the loop, next to mine. I'll hang onto you until you're stable."

With shaking hands Hiram did what John asked. He complained, "You're pushing too hard against me. It hurts."

"Better I should shove my body into you and the cliff wall, than chance you slipping over the edge."

For a moment, Hiram stopped whining.

John looked for a way up. Hiram spoke again, "You should have taken me first."

John ignored him. A light rain washed his face. He blinked to clear his eyes. He felt moisture soaking the rope. His hand slipped. He gripped harder.

Above him Moana's voice asked, "Are you Melody?"

"Look below you," John shouted.

Moana peered over the cliff's edge. "See you, brah." He blew on his conch shell again and again. "I think Al's coming. I can hear his cymbals clashing like crazy."

Akaka came to the edge of the precipice joined by two other men. "This is going to be tricky, touch-and-go."

"Hiram's fainted and can't help. Drop another rope with a noose on it. I'll put it around us, then you can haul us up."

Though John needed help, he realized that fear controlled Hiram. Barely had he secured Akaka's rope around them when the queen's courtier awoke. He screamed, flailed his arms, and tried to crawl over John's head. His sudden outburst loosened John's hold on his rope and they swung off the ledge.

Akaka's cord went taut, scraping dangerously over rocks as the two men swung pendulum-like over the cliff.

"Stop the swing before it cuts the rope," Akaka yelled.

John grabbed Hiram's neck. "You will die if you don't stop fighting me."

The crazed man ceased his struggles. John's feet found hard rock. "Pull us up!"

Chapter 11

The rescue successful, Hiram and Melody were turned over to a search party from Waimea. Faint light dimmed the horizon. "Too dark to attempt a slide down the mountain," Akaka said. "We find a spot to sleep and go tomorrow."

The four men made camp. Soon Moana had a fire, enough heat to ward off the early evening chill. Akaka pulled out some jerked meat and dried fish. The men sat and chewed on the salt-flavored, sun-dried morsels, and shared stories.

"I heard you arguing with Haku about an uhane and kahuna. What's what?" Akana asked.

"Old guy shows up out of the shadows and says there's a ghost haunting where we live. My father-law bought his claim hook, line, and sinker. I told him we are supposed to be Christians, not buy into that humbug stuff."

"Eh, we from Kau. We believe in the kahuna even if John no longer does," Moana interjected as Eleu nodded in agreement.

"But we are supposed to end black magic thinking. The queen ordered us to be Christians and give up on the old religion."

"Kaahumanu has been dead a long time," Akaka interjected. "The new king is turning back to the old ways."

"Do you really believe a kahuna can control the spirit of the dead and send it off on an evil mission to harm you?" John scoffed.

"Sure thing," Eleu answered. "When I was a little boy. A kahuna got a dead body. Cleaned it up for burial. Then said prayers and made strange sounds. Pretty soon I heard a whistling. The sound spun around the priest's grass shack several times then flew off into the mountains."

"What my cousin says is true," Moana said. "Kahuna tell me everyone has a spirit that separates from the body at death. This uhane can be captured and made to do bad things like go into someone and make him sick. My relative no feel good. He has chills in the feet, cold spreading up. Haku say, 'That's how uhane works.' If no do something quick he will die."

John's teeth tore into a stick of brown dried fish. He relished the morsel for a moment, staring at Moana. "No way can it happen. My grandfather fought with King Liholiho to overthrow the idols, destroy the temples where people were sacrificed to god Ku. Christians came and brought with them a god of goodness. No more shall we die by the false power of the kahuna."

"Eh, brah," Eleu interjected. "I know what I heard. What I saw."

"Did you see the uhane?"

"No way. Only the kahuna can see him."

"That's what I'm trying to say. The kahuna tells you, 'Only I can see the uhane.' And you believe him. He tells Haku an evil spirit haunts our land, and you believe this is why cousin is sick. The man preys on your fear of the old gods by what he claims to be true."

"Akaka, you've lived on the north shore a long time. Is there an evil uhane at Wainini?" Moana asked.

The fire blazed high, its bursting light creating eerie images in the trees surrounding the camp. Al stoked the fiery branches with a long stick and cast more brush onto the growing flames. "This is an argument that no side can win. Everything we know about the uhane comes from the kahuna. All we know of the Christian God comes from missionaries who claim he exists. None of us has seen either one. I have accepted Christianity even if I don't know God is real. It is much better to believe in one Lord of goodness than to obey many kahunas who frighten you with the fear of death."

"But cousin is sick. How do you explain it?"

"I cannot. Yet to believe that there are kahunas who cause death, or sickness, or possession of your body, or injury to it, I will not accept. John is right, when Liholiho destroyed the idols and the temples and did not die, the power of the old beliefs ended. It is much better now. A kahuna can no longer order a kapu which to break it means death. I know old beliefs are slow to pass away. I accept that. You should accept that John and I embrace the new religion."

Moana shrugged. "Okay, I hear you, but Haku and Momma will not change."

"Okay, enough talk, finish eating, and go to sleep. We have a long day ahead of us."

The company on the crest of the Wainiha ridge settled down to sleep. The fire burned low. Suddenly a powerful wind blew through the valley below. It flowed over the Alakai swamp. The embers of the fire burst into a crackling fountain of sparks. The sudden light woke John. He thought he saw in the rising flames the face of a woman, hair billowing out around her face. *It must be a dream,* he thought. *It cannot be Pele.* He fell back to sleep.

Pele

Chapter 12

It took the Akaka group two days to return to Wainini Beach. The trek down the mountain proved difficult. The ocean currents and winds sweeping along the coast slowed their canoe to a crawl.

When he finally arrived at the family compound, John was angered to learn that Haku Alapai left offerings at the altar. He stifled his protests to avoid an argument that would create an inseparable breach between the two men.

Mahealani came and snuggled into him. "Hungry? Come eat."

In the kitchen food lay spread out on the table. She gave him strong tea. John drank and suddenly stopped. "It tastes like it's full of ape."

"Drink, it will make you love me with an insane passion."

"What is this?"

"What the kahuna gave me. Marry me, I want you."

"What did you give him in return?"

Mahealani hung her head, crying.

John stormed from the shack, uncontrollable emotions welling within him. *What is tormenting me? The near-death struggle on the mountain? Belief in God or the kahuna?* John uttered these questions as he ran along the trail leading to Akaka's home. As he struggled with his feelings he realized that none of these things had provoked his outburst. *The words: 'Marry me, I want you.' had triggered an awful pain within.* He had lost land and love.

Auntie Malia's last words haunted him: "What the Hawaiian man got?"

"Nothing," John yelled to the sky.

He reached Akaka's home. Al took him in without a word, noting John's face. During his visit, he practiced Zen sitting on the highest hill overlooking Kalihiwai Bay. After several days of meditating, a messenger arrived inviting the two men to the home of the manager of Kilauea Plantation to meet the governor of Kauai. By that time, John believed he had cleansed his mind of the loss of his land and his love for Leinani. He decided what he must do. Happy, he trekked with Akaka toward the mill town.

As they neared the manager's home John recognized a black phaeton rolling out of the driveway. He glimpsed a face that existed only in his dreams. He broke into a run. The carriage sped away. A man next to Leinani drew her into him.

The wall John had built broke. "No!" he yelled.

The phaeton rolled rapidly away. Akaka came to John's side. "She is the one you have been grieving over."

"Yes."

They walked onto the driveway and entered the manager's house. A small party was in progress. Governor Kane praised the Akaka rescue team as heroes. Dowager Queen Emma was especially thankful to John for saving Melody and Hiram. She wanted to bestow a special gift upon him and had learned of Reverend Will's opposition to John's marriage. She had prevailed upon the cleric to perform the wedding and afterward she would give the greatest party that Kauai had ever seen. "Are you agreeable?" the governor asked.

John shuffled his feet as Kane finished. He looked at the governor, the plantation manager, and asked, "There was a black coach that left your home just as I came. I thought I recognized the woman in it. Who was she?"

The manager broke into a broad smile. "That was Mrs. James Kingsley. Leinani is her first name. The Kingsleys were just married. They ended their honeymoon here and are heading back to Honolulu. She is a stunning beauty. Are you acquainted with her?"

"Yes," John said, his voice quavering. He paused for some moments, fighting the emotions that shriveled his soul.

Then he said, "Tell Queen Emma I accept."

Chapter 13

Honolulu

Robert Grant snipped the end of his tightly wrapped cigar. He lit it and drew in a lungful of the aromatic weed. He studied his yearly ledger, burnt ash falling onto the pages. A knock at his office door disturbed him. He refused to answer the rapping, hypnotized by the revelation of the year's profits he had made from his sugar holdings.

Irritated, as the rapping came again, he uttered a curt, "What is it?"

"Sorry to disturb you, sir," an office clerk apologized, "but you wanted to be immediately informed when Mr. Larsen or Mr. Kingsley arrived."

"Who's here?"

"Mr. Larsen."

"Send a boy to Mr. Kingsley's home and learn if he will attend me or I should come to him. Let Larsen in, but interrupt us should my son-in-law arrive."

Within moments, the giant Swede entered with a broad smile on his face. "You seem unusually happy," Grant groused.

"Da man, he like hypnotized." Larsen raised his eye brows and winked.

Perturbed by what he perceived as insolence by an underling, Grant snapped, "What do you mean by that?"

The smirk left Larsen's face, "Sorry S.s.sir. You say watch them on honeymoon. First few days never leave the house. When finally go out man can't keep hands off woman. Rub back, stroke bottom, kiss, kiss."

"Your meaning is, he's in love with her"

"Yah, for sure. He hooked."

Grant's usual sour expression turned into a smile. Kingsley would refuse Leinani nothing, and as her father he could never say no to his requests. His smile broadened as he thought of the possibilities.

He studied Larsen for a few moments. The man looked away, shifting in his seat. "What about John Tana?"

"No show up. Woman visited taro fields. Stared at every man. Went to beaches, searched. If she finds him, I kill. But no show."

Grant nodded. "He is on that island somewhere. Did either of them see you?"

"No sir. I hide from them good."

"What did you learn about the plantations?"

"Princeville in valley. Plenty rain. Not good. Other plantation higher up. They can make it. Smart move, buy land along Kilauea River. Own the water."

There was a knock at the door.

"What is it?"

The office clerk looked in. "Boy is back. Kingsley is on his way."

"Good. Larsen, go. I don't want you around when my son-in-law comes. I'll call for you later."

The big Swede left. Grant puffed at his half-smoked cigar, contemplating what his underling had said. He moved to an office window watching the parade of people outside. *Could I gain control of the sugar mills in north Kauai? What would Kingsley tell me?*

Footsteps approached the door. He rushed to it and opened it with a flourish. A beaming young man reached out his hand. Grant ignored it and grasped his son-in-law to his chest. "Delighted to see you my boy. Your holiday exquisite?"

Kingsley stammered, "It-it-it, it was a glorious vacation. Your daughter is beyond doubt the most stunning beauty ever created. Her female charm made me giddy with desire for her."

"Did I tell you the truth about her virtue?"

"Oh yes, there was blood on the sheets after our first love making."

"Good. It would be indelicate of me to pursue the subject further. It is enough to know that I did not deceive you about my child."

"You did not. I want you to know, I could speak of my love for her forever."

Grant clipped a cigar and then another, offering one to Kingsley. He lit both then asked, "You found time I trust to investigate the mills?"

"In between our visits to mud fields and beaches, yes. I spoke to the manager of Kilauea, a Scotsman. He's partnered with another Scot and an Englishman. He is excited by the opportunity the reciprocity treaty with America provides entrepreneurs like him and his associates."

"What about the land?"

"He was euphoric. Rich soil. Plenty of water from the river. Sugar cane will grow in the uplands. It is not like Hanalei valley where Princeville's mill operates. Too much rain creates ponds of mud."

Grant inhaled a lungful of cigar smoke and slowly breathed it out enjoying the bite on his tongue and the aroma he exhaled. "What about investing on the north shore?"

"Princeville is not a good choice. Kilauea is worth considering. They have formed a stock company. I loaned them money for equipment at a good rate. They are friendly to me and we can buy shares at a decent price. What say you?"

Grant shifted in his chair. He put his stogie in an ash tray. "What you propose is interesting. Let's see how negotiations progress for a reciprocity treaty. Our new king has gone to Washington with control of Pearl River as his trade bait for an agreement."

"Do you think Kalakaua will fail to make a deal with America for the finest naval base in the Pacific?"

Grant studied his fingernails. "Let's just say it would be foolish for that country not to agree, especially if they want to control trade with Asia. Japan is just becoming an empire since the end of the Shogun wars. Britain is engaged in remaking India after the rebellion. France has been beaten by Prussia and is no longer a major player. Chancellor Bismarck, of a newly united Germany, is not interested in colonialism. Now is the time for America to make its move for domination in the Pacific while other world powers are distracted."

Strasbourg, France

Seventy-five-hundred miles away in Strasbourg, a French war veteran, Joe Still, finished packing his bag. He kissed his mother goodbye, embraced his father, and went into the night. At the railroad station, he spied a poster. In the dim light, he read: "Able-bodied men between 18 and 26 will report for registration at the nearest prefecture".

Still moved into the shadows and watched the railroad platform for anyone in a pickelhaube helmet. He knew a Prussian official would stop him for questioning, but a French gendarme in a braided hat would let him pass. It was hard for him to believe the Prussians had beaten the French and now controlled the area.

Two soldiers paced the lighted quay in front of him. They swiveled their heads from left to right, searching. A strident whistle announced the coming of a passenger train. Did he dare make a move toward the stairs to the platform? Still paused, watching the officials. They had stopped in their walk and stood surveying the area around them.

Still had hoped there would be a crowd of people at the station. Only a few awaited the train. He needed a distraction, but what could it be? Maybe he should follow his alternate plan, run and jump onto the train once it left the platform. He knew it would be dangerous, especially with his heavy bag.

Should he wait? Not a good option. He had delayed too long in Strasbourg. The conscriptors would come knocking any day now, looking for him. Fight for Germany? Never.

With a shriek of grinding iron, the dark locomotive pulled into the station. Still knew it would wait only a few moments to allow passengers off and others on. He watched the soldiers. They stood immobile. They did not study who came from the wagons, but who waited to get on.

Travelers descended the stairs heading for the street. Still shouldered his bag, climbed the steps, mixing as best he could with those leaving the train. He watched the officials. One began to turn in his direction.

What to do? Bend low? Retreat? He adjusted the brim of his hat.

"You, stop!"

Still froze, almost knocked off the stairs by a departing traveler. He glanced at the soldiers. They were looking away at someone else who was trying to get on. Without hesitating, Still shouldered his way through the people leaving, heaved his bag onto the floor of a passenger coach, and pulled himself in.

Finding a seat, he collapsed, allowing the pumping of his heart to slow its wild pace. There would be a border checkpoint to deal with. He had a plan for that. For the moment, he had escaped conscription by the new German army which someday would fight another war against France.

Chapter 14

Kauai, 1877

John Tana poled his canoe over the reefs. From a small gourd, he flicked coconut oil across the water's surface. Where the liquid landed, the sea became glass-smooth and he could search the coral bottom for the telltale signs of the octopus: disturbed rocks, black sand, empty shells.

A hundred feet away John saw Mother Alapai standing in shallow water. Her body leaned toward the deep channel that bordered the reef, a hand waving in the air. John nearly returned her wave before he realized that she was signaling in panic. Her forehead lay on top of the water.

John pushed his dugout toward the old woman. When he reached her, Alapai's face was submerged and air bubbles danced around her hair. Slimy grey-brown tentacles twined about her neck, their sucking cups holding fast to her throat. In the clear water, John saw an enormous octopus dragging the woman into the channel. He leaped from his craft, swam to his mother-in-law's side, and thrust his knife into the creature's mottled head.

The animal's color changed from streaks of dark brown and grey to deep purple. A tentacle lashed at John seeking his face, a slippery finger entering his nose. He ignored the attack and sliced at the slimy arms that held the old woman, then used his free hand to push her upward, forcing her nose and mouth from the sea. He stabbed the bulbous head of the beast as a second tentacle slid against his throat, coiling around it like a snake.

He shook his head to free it of the twining arms. John continued to thrust his knife until purple ink fogged the water and the octopus released its grasp. John lifted Mother Alapai from the sea and stumbled along the coral to his drifting dugout. There he worked to revive her until she coughed and water ran from her mouth.

When he brought her to the family compound, questions were asked, but John could only relate what he saw. The old woman kept saying, "Big head. Poke with spear, then, all bad..." Haku Alapai believed the attack had supernatural implications and sent for a kahuna living beyond Anini stream.

John protested, "This is nonsense."

"You are wrong," Mahealani answered with a vehemence that surprised him. "Only the kahuna can give us the answer to this attack. The octopus was bewitched by an enemy."

John took a deep breath, wanting to argue with Haku and his wife, but he knew it to be useless. He remembered his protests to the giving of offerings to a shaman. It had nearly destroyed his relationship with the Alapai family. Fortunately, the ana ana had been found dead at his altar. He thought the death would have ended the paganism of the family, but today *he realized that the dark arts of the kahuna were more persuasive than all my arguments of the goodness of God.*

While he waited for the woman to arrive, a messenger came from Akaka: John is needed at Kalihiwai Bay. A school of big-eyed skad is moving shoreward.

John raced along Wainini Beach, up a low hill, and swam across the Kalihiwai River. Fishermen working on nets waved to him as he hurried along a curving beach. He came to a black cliff wall which he climbed, finally reaching an eroded orange hill overlooking the bay.

A deep bass voice boomed, "Hui, John, why are you wearing red shorts? You know the shark god hates fishermen who wear red."

"Hui yourself. You're a superstitious old fool. That pagan stuff is nonsense."

Akaka rose from a rock seat and joined John at the edge of the orange plateau. "Al, you're always looking for signs of misfortune. But if you're interested in a good omen look at this spider web, it's filled with rainbows of dew. That means we'll have good luck today."

Akaka nodded. "I always like to keep the gods happy when I fish, the Christian God and the Hawaiian. I hope you're right about the spider web, because I've been watching a dark red spot just beyond the shore. For a week it has wandered close, yet too far for our nets to reach. This morning, I saw streaks of red darting in many directions."

John understood that predators were striking the scad and forcing them into shallower water. He stared into the bay. The sun shone on the waters. It highlighted a large, dark ball. Reddish streaks flashed outward from the sphere then back into the clump, like a fist opening and closing.

Al raised ti leaves over his head and waved them in a circling pattern toward the sea. "Go to the beach. The boys will be going out. The fish are coming in and we're going to catch them."

John scrambled down the hill. Behind him Akaka yelled, "Take off those red shorts and show you're a man, hah."

John slid onto the beach and ran to men pushing a net-filled rowboat and a canoe into the sea. He joined three of them wrestling the bigger craft into the surf. As a cresting wave lifted the vessel's bow, John seized the port-side wale, leaped in, grabbed an oar, and pulled out to sea.

Ito, a Japanese handyman, Cabral, a Portuguese sailor from the Azores, and a nephew of Akaka made up the crew. John watched Al's ti leaf signals directing his teams. A canoe zipped by them with two men paddling while a third payed out net, one end on shore held by two women. Several elderly Hawaiians strolled towards the breaking surf, where they waited until asked to join in the work of pulling in the net.

On the crest of the hill, Al waved the ti leaf branches seaward, and the canoe and rowboat raced into blue water. "Canoe out of net," John said. "Pull over."

Akaka waved frantically on his hillside perch. John knew he was anxious, concerned that the scad would escape. "Everybody go easy while we seam nets together. Ignore Al. When we ready, we ready."

"Everything tied together," Ito said.

"Let's go," John ordered, pulling hard on the oars while Ito payed net into the sea.

"The water is too deep. Float line going under the surface," Ito moaned.

John stared at Al on the hill. "The guy wants us to row further out to sea! The fish will just swim over the net."

"Signal him we got to turn in," Ito said.

"He's signaling 'no, go further out'. It must be a huge school of fish."

"We go out further we surround nothing."

"He's signaling a turn. Pull hard everybody."

The rowboat sliced through the water broadside to the waves. They smashed against the vessel, rocking the boat from side to side. "Cabral, bail, before we sink," John ordered as water from a rogue wave washed into the boat.

John glanced ahead and saw surf smashing into the promontory that channeled the Kalihiwai River into the sea. "We're going to crash into the rocks," Cabral yelled.

John glanced at the hill. Akaka waved them toward the promontory. "The fish must have drifted close to the rocks. We got to keep going. Everybody be ready to turn."

Ocean spray flew above the headland showering the men with seawater. Moments before impact, John saw Akaka's signal. "Turn, turn."

Wood scraped onto stone, timbers groaned, water seeped into the boat. "Row, row," John yelled, sweeping his oar into the sea, hauling it through with all the power he possessed. Net flowed out. A wave built up behind and roared toward the shore. It lifted the boat and hurled it at the beach. The last of the net fell into the roiling water, fifteen feet from shore. John leaped overboard, grabbed an end rope attached to the net, and searched with his feet for a sand bottom. Finding nothing to stand on, he swung the rope around his chest and side-kicked toward shore. Ito came beside him, helping to pull. The rowboat gyrated in the waves, the two men in it struggling to gain control before it floundered.

A few feet from shore, the rope jerked against his chest and John knew the net had snagged on rocks. "Ito, hang on. Pull as I free net. Yell for help."

John dove, feeling the strands of netting, searching for the snag. Net billowed around him, threatening to envelop his body like a shroud and roll him onto the boulders. His hand found net trapped by a protruding stone. He worked quickly, but could not free it. He tried to surface. The net held him under. His body was rolled onto the rocks by a large wave crashing into the promontory. With a sharp jerk, the trapped mesh came free. John thrust his head above the roaring sea, gulping air. He pushed away from the dark boulders yelling, "Ito, pull."

Men on shore came into the water to help the Japanese. They dragged the net to the beach. The fish were trapped. Akaka ordered a second surround of them.

"Big catch," John said as a mass of squirming fish was drawn to the shore.

Akaka reached into the jam of animals, seized a tail, and heaved a thresher shark into the nearby shrubbery. He pulled out more sharks. He waved to some Chinese huddling nearby. "Come, make fin soup." They hurried to the pile of predators and hauled them away.

As he assembled his crew, Al said, "We leave the second net in place. It will be our storage locker until the rest of the fish are needed. Go check the net for breaks and repair them."

John swam along the outside edge of the second net and saw a long rent. He called to a nearby canoe, retrieved a bone needle and a length of fiber from it. He hyperventilated, dove, and sewed the gaping hole together. It was difficult work when the ocean's surge stretched the torn ends apart, forcing him to pull them back together.

On his second dive, the net billowed over him. Startled, John looked up and saw a mass of scad pushing mesh over his head as they tried to escape. He struggled upward, but the webbing entangled him. Unable to free himself, John fought panic. He asked for God's help, but seconds passed and he remained trapped.

He remembered the words of his father, *"When in trouble in the sea, pray to your aumakua,"* on that day long ago when they were far out. His father chummed the water with bags of offal, then slit open fish and dumped entrails into the ocean, calling to the shark god. A huge predator came, circling their canoe. His father cut John's hand, letting blood drip into the empty stomachs of the slit fish. Then he threw his offerings to the tiger shark and said as the creature fed, *"He is now your personal god. When you need him, ask your aumakua for help."*

Desperate, John prayed to the god.

With a violent jerk, the cord webs pulled away from his body. The mass of fish that had caused the net to balloon over him fled toward the shore. John felt his toes and fingers come free of the mesh, and he kicked toward the surface, his body brushing by the white underbelly of a massive creature. Spasms wracked his lungs, lights darted, his mouth opened. John knew he would drown if he breathed underwater. Despite the need, he clamped his jaw shut.

With a dolphin kick, John thrust upward. Like a harpooned whale, he breached the surface, gulped air, and fell back into the water. Several feet from him a long, grey shape floated near the net. With a wag of its dorsal fin, the great shark moved out to sea, and John knew that his aumakua had smashed into the billowing net, frightened away the scad, and saved his life.

When he reached shore, laughter greeted him. A naked child waddled toward him. Behind his son, Mahealani held their three-year-old daughter, Nani.

"Oho ea," John called, swinging his giggling child over his shoulders.

"*Oho ea*," Mahealani answered.

They exchanged breath, their children nestled between them. John did not mention his prayer to the shark god. It worried him that when the Christian God failed him, he had turned to the old beliefs. He knew Mahealani would take his salvation as an omen for the family to return to the religion of the kahuna.

"The food is ready," his wife said, escaping John's embrace. "Come with me, some Chinese men want to meet you."

Within the pinewood forest that grew beyond the beach, a cauldron bubbled above an open fire. From the bowl came the aroma of sugar-sweetened soy sauce mixed with ginger. Mahealani led John to one of the men working nearby. "Sui Young, this is my husband, John. You asked for him earlier."

"Ayah, you friend of Muk Fat?"

John nodded.

"Muk Fat say you friend of Chinese, plenty big help to us. We same family from China." Sui Young pointed out people working near the stove. "Hulan Company send us to plant rice in Hanalei. We like make friend with Hawaiian, be *aikane*." He looked hopefully at John.

"Yes, we are aikane." John extended his hand and they shook on their friendship.

"Come. We celebrate. Eat shark fin soup, great delicacy—" Young stopped speaking when John coughed.

"I offend? I so sorry."

John waved away the apology, unable to speak.

The Chinese apologized yet again, his eyes filled with concern. "Mr. Tana, maybe you come see me in Hanalei? We want talk with you."

John nodded his agreement when Sui Young suggested they meet in two days. The Tana family bid farewell and moved toward the *luau* getting underway in the pine forest.

Maheaiani led them to a table set next to a pathway that bordered the trees. Akaka stood at the edge of the forest, tending a makeshift bar. Several men and a woman were drinking with him. In clear spaces within the woods, large mats were spread on the ground and women moved back and forth, carrying bowls of food and placing them upon the mats. A dozen kukui nut torches were speared into the sand surrounding the eating area.

On the beach, a bundle of wood blazed. A man ignited a torch from it and loped through the pinewoods lighting the kukui brands. Soon, the forest glowed with orange-yellow light filtering through the tall, slender pines. Above Kalihiwai Bay, the sky blazed a brilliant crimson. Akaka motioned John to join him at the bar.

"Meet Leong Wong, the richest Chinese orphan to come to Hawaii, and this is Robert MacDuff, Manager of Princeville Plantation. To your left is Paul Eisner, a wealthy sugar planter, and next to him is our new Governor, Paul Kalakou. Gentlemen, meet John Tana, the bravest and strongest man in all of Kauai. Mr. MacDuff, if you need protection for your operations, he is the one who can do it for you."

Al's bragging embarrassed him. But John knew his friend meant well. They had discussed finding work on the north shore, but other than laboring in the sugar fields, a job he hated, there was no other employment for a Hawaiian.

"Mr. Tana not only appears strong, but he is quite good looking as well," a woman said. "In fact, as I look more closely, his cropped brown locks, those penetrating eyes, that fine nose and full lips, I must say that he is very handsome." Before anyone could respond, she smiled broadly. "I wonder if he's a Lothario or an Othello."

John knew the woman thought him to be an ignorant savage, that she was intent on destroying any chance that he might have of gaining employment in a world controlled by those who were white. He noted Akaka fidgeting, unable to stand still, a look of worry on his face. John wished her words away, but it was clear that this group of important people were awaiting his response. He saw their expressions, felt their amusement. After all, what could a native know about the civilized world of playwrights and literature? John was grateful that Mahealani had brought him a blouse and pantaloons to cover his nakedness. At least he had a civilized look, even though his insides quaked

John stood puzzled for a moment, searching the past. *His mind dwelled on remembrances from a world he once lived in with Leinani. For countless hours, they had discussed books she had read.* His brow furrowed, John faced his tormentor. "I'm not sure if you're talking about Don Quixote's friend or some other seducer." He saw her eyes widen in surprise, and he rushed ahead. "But I can tell you this: the black Duke of Venice I am not."

Paul Eisner chuckled, extending his hand. They shook. "Well done, young man. I knew there was more than one Lothario in literature, but you're saying that Cervantes had one in his magnificent story? I didn't know that. Did you, June?" Without waiting for an answer, he added, "And I agree with you, Mr. Tana, that you are nothing like Shakespeare's overly jealous Moor. Come, join us in a drink."

At Akaka's makeshift bar, conversation turned to security in the rice fields and at plantation properties of Kilauea and Princeville. Leong Wong mentioned that several different tongs, Chinese gangs, had occupied parts of Hanalei to plant rice. "This is a significant export from Hawaii. Many Chinese are working in California and require rice." He went on to say that competition between tongs was not achieved through cost-cutting, but by gang warfare. John learned that a week before, an artesian well owned by a group of Chinese had been destroyed, earthen embankments dug up, and their rice fields trashed.

"It's a problem for the sugar business as well. Survey markers were non-existent a few years ago. Today, whether the land is used for rice or sugar, encroachments are commonplace," MacDuff said.

"The pending warfare between the tongs threatens to spill over into the plantation work force," Eisner added. He went on to explain that there had been a marked increase in the theft of metal, especially knives. "Fortunately, all the firearms are accounted for and under lock and key."

"True," MacDuff said. "But no one can be sure what weapons the tongs have imported."

"I don't have enough police," Governor Kalakou complained. "The day has come when the people living on the north shore must solve their own security problems."

John listened quietly to the discussion.

"Do you have an interest in working with the plantation, in charge of security?" Macduff asked.

John thought about this for a long moment. "My wife wants to move to Hanalei, where there is a school for the children. I haven't been trained as a policeman, but I have served in the Honolulu militia and I know hand-to-hand combat. Mr. MacDuff, when can we meet?" The two men set a date. John thanked the others for their hospitality, and joined his family.

An old man called everyone to the beach fire where there would be music, singing, and hula. John and Mahealani gathered the children and joined other parents who brought their sleeping or protesting offspring to a house that sat inland from the beach. Mahealani placed sleeping Nani and John Jr. on the floor mats of the home. It was next to an ancient rock temple. With guardians watching over the children, the adults returned to the beach.

The Portuguese fisherman, Cabral, played his *bragina* and sang about a whaler far from home yearning for the woman he loved and hoped she was waiting for him to return. A few women stood and began to dance the hula, swishing and swaying to a rhythmic chant. Not to be outdone, several men rose and began their own wild songs filled with innuendo and raucous suggestions. Laughing, the women joined in with sexy dancing, keeping the men away with sudden hip movements.

The party continued into the night and, during a lull, John spotted Mahealani's sister, Puarose, who had remained in Wainini for most of the day caring for her mother.

"What did the kahuna say?" John asked.

"She wanted to know if you saw anyone on the bluff during the fight with the octopus."

John thought about this for a moment. "There was a man on the hill. After the octopus smeared the water with ink, he left."

"Oh, my, the kahuna is right. She said that the octopus is the aumakua of an enemy of Anahai and he sent his god to attack her. The man on the hill must be that enemy."

Mahealani heard her sister's words and wailed, "Oh, woe is us. Mama has offended a kahuna. Has she felt the coldness in her toes?"

"Stop this nonsense. You know that the Bible says: 'I am the Lord thy God, thou shall not have false gods before me'."

"What is this arguing about false gods?" Akaka asked, striding up to the three people.

"It's not really an argument," Puarose said. "It's just that John doesn't believe in the power of the kahuna."

"I'm a Christian. We don't believe in Kanaloa, Lono, Kane, Ku. We believe in one God."

"Ah, that is so," Akaka said, "but it was not too long ago," he pointed to a pile of rocks on a low mound, "that priests of Ku practiced their devil arts and sacrificed humans to the war god in that temple. Old beliefs die hard. Even today I can hear the voices of the dead whispering from those stones. Like you, John, I am a Christian. Mahealani and Puarose, banish your fearful thoughts. Give up your belief in the old religion. It is just black magic, without any truth to it."

John watched the expressions on the faces of his wife and sister-in-law. He noted their disagreement. They remained silent as he escorted them back to the party, his head filled with thoughts of his family and superstition. Before long, the dancers, singers, and musicians were exhausted, and couples drifted from the bonfire, seeking shadowy places to talk.

A light rain misted the valley. The moon shone silver upon the temple of rocks sitting on the low hill. From the door of the sleeping house adjacent to it, John heard blood-curdling shrieks and recognized the voice of his son. "Momma, help me! The uhane is coming to get me!"

John raced into the house and found his boy trembling with fear, wailing about a ghost coming to take him in the night.

Chapter 15

Hanalei Taro Field

At the northern margin of the tropics, in a belt of persistent trade winds, the great shield wall of Waialeale volcano thrusts above the Pacific Ocean. Wind, rain, fast-flowing water, carved from the volcanic rock a perfect valley and bay, rounded like the imprint of a giant's thumb pushed into green clay. Billions of tiny yellow grains of sand form a crescent beach that gives the place its name, Hanalei, necklace bay.

Perched on an overhang, John gazed into the valley. Cool air, suggesting the coming of rain, ruffled his hair. *The heavens always cast their water on Hanalei,* he thought, as he watched the clouds shrouding the top of the dead volcano.

A great black nimbostratus cloud wall drifted over the ocean, pushed by strong trades. Patches of blue sky disappeared as the massive blanket of rain blotted out the sun's rays, casting everything into depressive shadows. As the light dimmed over the valley, John scowled.

Once hundreds of thousands of Hawaiians lived in the islands, with more than fifteen thousand prospering in Hanalei. He imagined ancient times when the valley floor was crisscrossed with embankments filled with water and growing taro, *just like my farm in my lost land in Kahului.*

Memories flooded over him, *the wonder days of my youth, when I stood in the mud of my family's taro fields. Deep green leaves, velvet to the touch, glinting bright in the sun, their tall stalks thrusting leafy tops against my shoulders. All around me the taro grew, surrounding me with lily-like fragrance, a sweet smell like no other. Taro is a plant essential to Hawaiian life. Every part of it, from root to green top, is used for food. It could live and grow in all kinds of conditions, drought or flood. Today,* John thought, *sugar cane and rice have replaced taro in Hanalei.*

John's thoughts shifted to the loss of hundreds of thousands of Hawaiian men and women suddenly dead from the diseases brought by the foreigners. *In Hanalei, only a few hundred of my people are still alive. As for the land: once productive, it became untended, wild, until the haole and Chinese came with their desire to make money through growing sugar cane and rice. They gave nothing to the Hawaiian but woe and death.*

Birds flitted and sang, swooping among great hau trees, their branches filled with leaves and flowers, causing them to bend over the river rolling toward the sea. Thousands of blossoms bobbed on the surface, a multitude of tiny yellow boats heading for the ocean, or toward the wharf of the sugar mill that rested on the east bank of the river.

His nemesis, King Sugar, ate up this spiritual place. Yet he knew that *greedy people would learn that Hanalei was not kind to sugar cane.* John smiled, thinking how a Scotsman had come to Hanalei to "live like a lord" and had been defeated by the elements. On death, he left a sugar mill deep in debt. It was sold at auction and its new owners were trying to make it profitable.

Smudging clouds wiped away the last of the blue sky. Rain darkened the ocean and moved onto land, pelting the beach. John stood from his perch and headed to the river. *How strange it is for me to be acting like a haole, pursuing money. How un-Hawaiian*, he thought. *For this to happen, I would have to blame Mahealani. She was the one who desperately wanted to come to necklace bay and send the children to the mission school.*

John stepped into the barge used to ferry passengers across the river. Beyond the far bank, he saw green fields of sugar cane and rice plants squashed down by the downpour. Working with the ferryman, he pulled on the rope used to thrust the vessel across the water. Safely on the other side, John walked on the road winding along the river. He espied Sui Young and several Chinese men ahead, their clothing soaked from the deluge. When they saw him, they bowed many times, bobbing like corks in roiling water. Sui Young rushed up and offered his umbrella. "Come into our compound, Honorable Mr. Tana."

John followed Young into a low-walled enclosure, the Princeville sugar mill and several processing sheds visible on the opposite bank of the river. He wondered if, when he finished his business with Young, he would have time to visit MacDuff.

The Chinese planter showed him into a building. As he entered, John heard the distant lowing of cattle. "There are cows in Hanalei?"

"Yes!" Sui Young said, anger rising in his voice. "Our enemy says it is wild cattle in the hills that trash our rice fields at night, but I know better. It is those dirty Hakka who seek to drive us out."

"Hakka, why do they want to rid the valley of your people?"

Young sighed. "Maybe you think Hakka want us out for rice money? Hakka hate my clan, the Punti."

John said nothing.

Sui explained, "The Punti were the first to live in Canton region of China. For a thousand years, Punti farmed the lowlands, built the towns, and lived together in peace. Hakka are barbarians. They come from the north, no culture. We make them live in hills, not in lowlands where Punti live."

"Perhaps your ancestors were asking for trouble when they kept the Hakka in the hills," John said, wagging a finger at his friend.

"We Chinese respect our elders. We do not blame them for what happened many years ago." Then he went on to explain about the Opium Wars, started by the British to gain power. When the emperor was defeated, the country became weak and vulnerable. A religious fanatic gained control and attracted followers, many of them Hakka. They recognized that with power came the opportunity for revenge. They turned on their Punti neighbors and millions died. When the emperor regained his authority, hatred remained between the two factions and an exodus took place. Many of the Chinese found work in the sugar fields, where they were paid slave wages. Once they finished their labor contracts, they left the plantations and some began planting rice in fertile valleys like Hanalei.

"So, what can I do for you?"

Sui looked around, as if unsure how to begin. Finally, he said, "We desperate. Only twenty of us, enemy has sixty. They raid our fields and destroy plants, destroy artesian well. Soon, since no police, they attack. We need help from Hawaiians, from strong man like you. Will you lead us?"

John stroked his chin as he contemplated this request. *These were foreigners who had taken over the taro fields to make money from rice not to share it with Hawaiians.* Except for his brief time on the docks, that is how he had lived his life, sharing and trading. Other than what he had been taught by Ah Sam, he had no concept of the value of money, or what his services might be worth. But Mahealani wanted to move to Hanalei; to do so, he needed money. He released a sigh and did it the Hawaiian way: he neither bargained nor made demands, but simply answered, "Yes, I will help you." In this answer, there was no expectation of reward, no request for compensation. He and Sui Young were friends, and that was sufficient. Before he left the compound, John asked Young to send a message to Akaka to meet them later that day.

Chapter 16

Hanalei taro fields where Chinese once grew rice.

Evening fell and the sun blazed brilliant colors as it descended behind the mountains of Haena. Heavy rain had greened the moss and shrubs clinging to the dark blue cliffs of Waialeale. Freshly fueled waterfalls cascaded in foaming sheets onto the rocks, pools, and streams at the base of the dead volcano. A giant rainbow haloed the valley, its myriad colors shimmering in the last rays of the sun. John watched it disappear as he ran toward the compound of Sui Young. From a distance, he saw the Chinese moving fretfully back and forth, glancing at the sky. Cathedral-tall clouds were sweeping toward Waialeale, and as he came up to the compound, he saw Sui trembled. Beyond him, a thin crescent of sun sparkled crimson, orange and yellow, then vanished.

From the opposite direction, Akaka came marching along the road, two Hawaiians beside him. When Sui realized that everyone had indeed arrived, his face brightened, as if to say that John would know how to end his nightmare.

What remained of daylight lit the undersides of clouds drifting over the hills. The grey darkness of evening veiled the sky. Unable to restrain his anxiety Young blurted out, "Mr. Tana, what we going do?"

John studied Sui's face and recognized desperation in his eyes. He signaled to Akaka and his companions to huddle with him, along with Young and eight men of his clan.

"For the next two to three nights there will be no moonlight," John said, his eyes on Young. "It will be a good time for the enemy to strike at your rice fields."

Akaka nodded. "So, do we attack them in the dark, when they strike? That's risky stuff!"

"Hear me out," John said. He took a stick and drew two wavy parallel lines in the dirt, and then drew twelve vertical lines between them. "This line," he said, "is the road that follows the Hanalei River where it flows to the sea. This other one," pointing to the second parallel line, "is the mountainside path on the west side of the Valley. Between them are the Hakka and Punti rice paddies. And these," he added, drawing vertical lines, "are the dirt embankments that separate the paddies."

"Fine," Akaka interjected. "We all know that paddies are blocks of water trapped by dirt, but what's the plan?"

"Be patient. You're the boss when it comes to fishing, but I'm the boss when it comes to fighting, got it?"

Sui Young looked from John to Akaka, as if fearful that his two allies would soon become enemies. Al's men, Kunani and Kaipo, remained quiet, as they observed the tension.

Akaka stared at John, his face rigid. Slowly it broke into a smile. "OK, you be the guy with the biggest muscles, the boss man of this fight, just so long as, when we go fishing, I'm the boss."

"Deal." John returned to his drawing. "The only good way for the enemy to get at the paddies is by the river road, or along the mountainside path. They know the road will be watched, so they'll use the path. At this location is a dip," John said and pointed to his diagram. "I've buried a long rope there, with each end attached to a pole. After the enemy raiders trash one of Young's rice fields —"

"Ayeeah," Young wailed. "No can lose more fields. Oh, woe is Hui of Sui Young."

"I'm sorry, but we need proof that it isn't wild cattle destroying your fields, but your enemy. The raiders will use the mountainside path to go south to attack your fields and they will use it to return to their compound."

Kunani interrupted, "I get it. When the raiders come to the dip, we yank the rope and they fall. But what if there are too many of them?"

"Our object is not to fight all the raiders, but catch two or three and drive away the rest."

Akaka asked, "But isn't this going to be tough at night? When it's dark we can't tell friend from foe."

John went forward describing his plan, then divided the men into three teams. The rest of the evening was dedicated to drills for the ambush.

After midnight, a Chinese brought news that the enemy moved south along the mountain to invade the rice fields of the Young hui. John gathered his fighting force. With weapons in hand they moved onto a large earthen embankment bordering the rice fields of the warring factions and headed west to its intersection with the hillside path.

Once there, John detailed his teams to their ambush positions. "Do not attack until I give the signal, *Imua i na poki*, 'go forward young brothers'. This is the battle cry of Kamehameha the Great."

John and a Chinese fighter crouched by an embedded pole in the embankment. He held a rope inserted into a ring fastened to the pole. The other end of the rope lay under a shallow layer of dirt and ran fifteen feet west along the causeway, across its intersection with the mountainside path, then fifteen feet further to a sister pole set into the hill.

In the rice fields to the south John heard thrashing water accompanied by low voices mumbling and calling. John did not attack. He wanted prisoners, not a night battle.

After a time, John heard voices moving north. He and his companion crawled closer to the intersection of embankment and path, the knotted rope in John's hand. He heard sounds of movement then shadowy figures walked by. He waited as the men descended into a dip then up again. Nine Chinese passed.

Three laggards approached the slope. John whispered to his companion, "Pull the rope." It became taut and the men fell headlong into the rice paddy.

"*Imua i na poki*," John signaled. Torches flamed over the mountainside illuminating the raiders.

John twirled his tripping cord and swung it. The weighted line wrapped around the legs of an enemy. He pulled and his adversary fell backward into the rice field. "Tie him up," he said to his companion. John leaped from the embankment into the mud attacking another enemy who had fallen into the wet earth. A hoe swung. John dodged the poorly aimed weapon and dealt the wielder a sharp rap on his head with a small club. The man fell into the muck. John grabbed his queue and hauled the unconscious Chinese onto the earthen dike.

Torches lit up the intersection of mountain path and dirt embankment. As John regained firm ground he saw Al and a helper had netted a third man. They faced two enemies attempting to aid their fallen companions. Ranged along the hillside, Kaipo, Kunani, and six Chinese holding long spears fought seven raiders armed with hoes.

John removed his sling from his head. He flung a stone at a man menacing Al. The rock glanced from the face of the Chinese.

"I kill you," he yelled, and charged.

John flung another stone. The Chinese howled and escaped into a rice paddy. Another stone knocked him to his knees.

Al's remaining opponent backed away, his hoe held out before him. John approached with his sling twirling. The Chinese man dropped his weapon and fled north. His sudden rush caused a panic and the remaining enemy also ran.

"Al, take charge of our three captives," John said. "I'm going after the last guy." He got a torch and raised it. At the edge of the light a man thrashed north in the muddy field.

John called, "Tell your head man I will visit him tomorrow."

Chapter 17

In the morning, John sent Al to the Hanalei Hawaiian village. Each prisoner had been isolated since their capture. John questioned them separately. By noontime he acquired all the information he needed. During lunch, he discussed his plan with Sui and Al who had returned. With some timing changes, the men agreed to John's proposal. Al left.

With the three captives, John and all of Young's men headed for the enemy village. As they approached the Hakka encampment, alarm bells pealed. Within minutes Chinese rushed in from the rice fields and assembled in their enclosure. Soon three men walked out.

John held up his hands, palms open. "Who is your headman?"

A stocky, bald Chinese stepped forward. "I am Li Lao Tse. Why you come here?"

"To talk peace in Hanalei Valley. We want your men to stop raiding the rice fields of Sui Young's hui."

Li took a step closer and spat at John's feet. "We not raiders. We peaceful. Maybe wild cows hurt fields."

John shook his head. "We caught three of your clan last night." He motioned for Kaipo and Kunani to bring forward the bound captives.

"I don't know these men."

"Really?" John replied, eyebrows arched. "So why did they all say that they belong to you? Look at the man by your side," he added, gesturing to a Chinese with a cut on his cheek. "That's where my stone hit him last night."

When there was no reply, John said, "It's time to talk peace. Are you willing?"

"You one dumb kanaka. We sixty men. You only twenty. We will cut off your balls and stick down your throat." Turning to his followers, Li pointed at John and his group. "Get these dumb asses!"

"Wait!" John's voice boomed. "Before you attack, see what's behind you."

Li looked back. A small army of Hawaiians, led by Akaka, marched up the river road, armed and ready to fight.

John saw defeat cross his opponent's eyes. "We have enough men to run you out of this valley. Sit with me and talk peace."

Li studied the marching Hawaiians and then turned back to John. "Maybe you got enough men to beat us, but you cannot defeat my kung fu. How about we go one-on-one, winner be boss-man in the valley?"

"Everybody should try to get along –"

Before John could finish, the headman ran forward, leapt high, his feet extended. John stepped into the attack and to the side.

As Li's body passed by, John delivered a vicious blow to his kidneys.

The headman gasped when he struck the ground, then rolled, came upright, and assumed a fighting stance. Left foot forward, right foot planted solidly behind him, arms upraised with palms open and fingers squeezed together.

For many moments, the two opponents faced each other. Li beckoned with his hand for John to come and take him out.

Silence.

"You dirty kanaka scared of me? You all talk. No good for shit. Come, let's see what kind of man you are. Try and take me out."

"It is up to you if we are to have war or peace between us. You must make the first move."

Li slid forward with his left leg. He planted it and pivoted, swinging his right foot in a sweeping motion aimed at John's kidneys.

John moved away from the sweep, but not fast enough. Li's shoe glanced against his side. With remarkable agility, the headman landed on his right foot, pirouetted about and struck John's thigh with his left foot.

John winced from the painful hit then smashed his fist into his opponent's back. The punch brought him to his knees, his arms outstretched as he pitched forward. Without pausing John leaped onto his antagonist's back sliding his right arm under Li's arm and onto his neck. With his left hand, John attempted to pin him, but was unable to do so. Li flailed about seeking to grab the back of John's head.

With his legs clamped around his opponent's torso, John applied his half-Nelson hold against his shaven skull. His adversary rolled, hurling John's body onto the ground.

Despite the sting of the fall, John maintained his steady pressure on the neck with his right hand and squeezed with his legs. As his opponent flailed, he gave John a momentary opening. He seized the opportunity to slide his left hand under the armpit and onto Li's head completing a full Nelson.

Two Chinese came forward to aid their stricken leader, but halted as Kaipo and Kunani cautioned them to stay out of the fight. Around the contestants, a wide ring of Hawaiians and Chinese formed.

"Best you stop before I break you," John said, his voice low and menacing. Li kept thrashing. John's arm muscles bulged. He applied vise-like pressure on the neck forcing his opponent's chin almost too his chest.

"Give it up. Let's talk peace."

Li could only gasp for air as the power of John's full Nelson prevented him from answering. Before the Chinese lapsed unconscious John released his hold and pushed away from him.

The stricken man groaned, vomited, and rolled onto his back. John looked at his enemies. "Do you want to fight or make peace?"

Several voices called out, "No fight, no fight."

John turned to Li's two companions standing near Kaipo and Kunani. "What is it going to be?"

"We no like fight. He head man. Must ask him what do. No fight. We take him to the shed over there. When better we call you to talk."

"Okay, but tell your men no make trouble or big angry. Tell them to break it up and go back to work."

Two Chinese helped their fallen leader to his feet. He shook his head and stared at John.

"Truce?"

There came a slow nod. "I…I must talk with Honolulu."

"We will go home. When you're ready, send word. Until then make no trouble. I will be watching."

It was late afternoon when John returned to the Punti compound. He decided to follow up on MacDuff's offer and headed across the river to the Princeville mill. A large barge stacked with cane was being unloaded at the pier. Chinese workmen scurried between the vessel and waiting wagons with loads of cut cane in their arms. John saw the small men panting under the strain of carrying the heavy bundles, the leaves on the stalks slicing into their flesh. *Such punishing work.*

John pushed his boat into the mud adjacent to the dock, and scrambled up the bank. A dozen men worked at hauling. John asked one of them where to find MacDuff. The man pointed in the direction of the mill. John trudged away from the dock, resenting the miserable work that these men had contracted to do, ten hours a day, six days a week.

Near the mill, he found a building marked 'Office' and entered. It was a sparse room, with deep brown walls and floor. At a desk, a Caucasian man wrote entries into a journal. He looked up when John came in. His face turned sullen, his body stiffened. "What do you want?" he asked, his voice surly.

"Mr. MacDuff asked me to stop by," John answered, his tone low and respectful.

The man stood eyeing John's muscular six-foot-two-inch frame, his plain tattered shirt, clean white loin cloth, and bare feet. "Name?"

"John Tana."

Holding out his palm in the universal symbol to wait, the man skirted his desk, walked to an inner door and knocked. There was a muffled answer, and the Caucasian entered the office. He could barely hear the words, "Half-naked kanaka…name's John Tana."

There was a brief conversation, then the Caucasian returned to his desk, waving his hand in dismissal. "Mr. MacDuff can't see you now. Where can you be reached?"

"The Chinese compound across the river."

"We'll send word when we want you," the man said, scorn in his voice. "Now go!"

Discouraged, John returned to the dock as workers drayed the loaded wagons to the mill. *I guess he didn't mean it. Maybe I should have worn better clothes.* John clenched his fists over his paddle, and forced his canoe across the river, wondering how he and Mahealani could find a way to send the children to the Mission school in Hanalei.

That night, there was a dinner honoring the four Hawaiians. Sui Young declared his gratitude. "Mr. Tana," he announced. "Without you our clan finished in Hanalei. For your work, you ask for nothing. You say friends help friends. I say you part of Sui Young hui. You get five percent of rice profits for being our guardian and keep peace."

John protested that it must be the wine and the happiness of the evening for Young to make such a generous promise. But Sui Young insisted, and John fell silent. He knew that the man was adamant, and arguing further might cause him to lose face. Next morning, John and his companions headed home. Young promised to send word once there was news from Li.

Chapter 18

Two weeks passed before a message came to return to Hanalei for a meeting. Although it stretched the family's finances to the limit, Mahealani acquired a new pair of dark pants, white shirt, and footwear for the occasion.

"This is not necessary," John protested.

"If you become a guardian of the valley you must look the part. And you don't know what may happen with the plantation."

"You're wrong, MacDuff has no interest in dumb Hawaiians."

"You told me you wished you had good clothes and shoes when you visited the manager. Maybe he would have been more interested if you looked better."

"I don't think so. His clerk didn't care for me. I'm sure his boss felt the same."

John dressed and joined up with Akaka, Kunani, and Kaipo. They headed for Hanalei.

The two Chinese leaders had set the meeting at Sui's compound. When the Hawaiians arrived, bargaining did not begin. Sui had already conveyed to Li what he had promised, and urged him to remind his superiors that John was a friend of the Chinese. At the meeting Li was the first to speak. With a white-toothed smile, he related that his employers knew of John's help to the Chinese community in Honolulu. Inquiry was made of the headman in the capitol and he confirmed, "Mr. Tana will be 'boss man' in Hanalei and receive five percent of rice profits to keep the peace."

Young threw a feast that night for the combined clans and the four Hawaiians. Influenced by rice wine and beer, everyone protested their friendship and welcomed peace. The Hawaiians sang ribald party songs with loud belting of the racy parts accompanied with winks and suggestive hip movements. John did not drink much, and left the party early, happy with the knowledge that Mahealani would get her wish. Behind, he left friends dancing a wild hula with the Chinese.

Chapter 19

"Fire! Fire! Help!" someone screamed.

The strident cry brought John awake and he scrambled outside. Through hau trees he could see ridges of red-orange flames stabbing into the night. Princeville buildings were blazing.

At the river's edge were boats loaded with Chinese men. John raced to a scow, jumped in, and helped the volunteer firefighters reach the northeastern bank of the river. Roiling smoke, dark as the night, shrouded the landing area and the ground around it. John scrambled up the earth bank. His feet slipped on soft mud. He saved himself from falling by grabbing a shrub and hauling himself onto solid ground. Wind-whipped flames blasted hot air onto his body. Sweat dripped over his face, stinging his eyes. He squinted through the haze seeking the mill's manager. He found him near the fire and hollered, "What do you want us to do?"

MacDuff appeared startled when he saw John but recovered and yelled, "Organize a bucket brigade. Throw water on the boiler house. It's burning fast. Find some men to pump water." With that, he pointed toward a shed. "Meet me there."

John spoke to Sui Young, "Get men from your hui. Take buckets, form two lines from the river to the fire."

Sui nodded and began organizing his team.

His eyes smarting from the billowing smoke, John found Al and two Hawaiians. He led them to the shed where MacDuff waited, lines of worry etching his face. Within the building stood a rolling fire engine that the five men hauled to the blaze. Akaka, Kunani, and Kaipo pumped the handles until water spewed from the fire hose. John directed the stream of water where MacDuff pointed. Burning wood sizzled, steam spiraled upward, but the fire continued to burn, consuming the timbers of the boiler room, turning them black as the flames devoured the dry wood.

Overcome by smoke, men dropped from the fire line. MacDuff came, screaming over the whipping hot wind, "We can't save the boiler house." He pointed to the smoldering trash house. "If that goes, the warehouses and sugar mill will be next. Chop it down. Make a fire break."

Despite his throbbing head, John organized a group of men to smash the building. Hot smoke blew over them and John heaved with coughing, his eyes smarting. Someone thrust a wet cloth into his hand and he bound it around his nose and mouth.

New flare-ups lit the sky from hot ashes falling on the trash house. Spears of flame stabbed him, singeing his hair and skin. Water doused over his body, stifling the embers that had ignited his clothes. He breathed in the moisture, felt his lungs clear of smoke, and returned to the work of destroying the trash house. Soon, a wide path grew between it and an adjacent warehouse. Hot embers kept descending onto the buildings, blown by the wind.

"Beat the fire down!" John yelled. "Get water. Throw it on the hot spots!"

What remained of the trash house collapsed, hot ash and splinters of glowing wood flew onto the warehouse and the men creating the fire break. John felt the intense pain of burning skin and tore the shirt from his body. He saw a finger of fire flickering at the base of the warehouse and stomped it out.

With buckets of water, wet blankets, and shoveled dirt, the firefighters stifled the burning wood. The flames slowly died out, and the remaining hot coals were extinguished. By dawn the fire had run its course. The boiling house and trash shed were smoldering ruins, but the firebreak had saved the sugar mill and the warehouses.

"Good work, Mr. Tana," a grimy MacDuff said. "Would you come over here please?"

John stared at the manager and thought: *How polite the man is now. Two weeks ago, he turned me away from his office and I left, believing I would never find work in a Caucasian world.* He shivered in the cool morning air as he approached Macduff.

"First, let me thank you for your help. Without your efforts, we could not have saved the mill."

John nodded.

"There's a possibility that arson caused this," MacDuff confided. "Maybe an unhappy employee or more likely someone from over the hill in Kilauea who is trying to buy this plantation cheap. We need security to guard against arson, thefts, and keep away unwanted people. Interested in a job?"

John accepted MacDuff's offer of Chief of Security for Princeville Plantation. The manager hinted that additional security work could occur.

As he hiked home John could not believe his good fortune. *Peacekeeper in Hanalei, Chief of Security at Princeville with a promise of more work. Mahealani could move the family to Hanalei. Nani and John Jr. would receive an education at the Waioli Mission School. Maybe I could save enough money to buy land.*

Chapter 20

Wailua Bay, Kauai, 1878

John stood near the large boulders of a great stone temple at the mouth of the Wailua River. He recalled stories of priests who fished for the giant ulua and then sacrificed it to the gods at the altar inside. He knew that if they failed to catch the fish, a person would be hooked by the mouth and sacrificed instead. *Over the ages,* he wondered*, how many lives had been taken to please the pagan gods and receive their blessings?*

As he studied the ancient stones, John imagined the chiefs and priests, their sacrifices completed, boarding canoes and paddling up the broad river. He visualized high lords landing where the waters shallowed then trekking up a slippery trail to the crest of the dead volcano.

John gazed over the tops of the great grove of royal palms that sheltered the home of the princess. Above the trees rose Nounou Mountain. He watched clouds blowing in from the sea, rising above the mound of rock and facing a greater challenge, the five-thousand-foot wall of Waialeale. Rain would fall in sheets as the water-filled vapors unloaded their liquid burden then allowed the clouds to cross the high point of the island.

What insane courage, John thought, *for these priests and chiefs to brave the falling water and high winds to reach the altar at the summit and the rippling pond which gave the dormant volcano its name. Once the group assembled at the crest they would make sacrifices to the gods. This was done despite the powerful winds that blew around them, threatening to hurl the men into a churning waterfall cascading thousands of feet over moss-covered rock and into a great pool. Despite the dangers, John knew that the ancients believed in appeasing the gods and receiving their blessings. It was worth any threat to their lives.*

Anxious, he searched the ocean for a vessel long overdue. The horses by his side clomped nervously, their hooves smashing the green seashore naupaka. Waves crashed onto the beach, the foaming water colored brown by dirt and sticks of hau wood shoved into the sea by the river. Finally, John spied the sails of a schooner beating against the wind as it drew around the headland that supported the decaying and neglected temple.

The sails were trimmed and a boat launched. John rushed to where the water met the sand and waited. Within five minutes, he helped King David Kalakaua out of the craft.

"I can get my feet wet."

"Wailua's waters shall never dampen your toes," John said, steadying the craft with his legs.

A wave crashed against the hull and Kalakaua teetered, his body angling toward the water that eddied around them. John heaved the portly man from the boat and carried him to dry land.

When the monarch stood safely ashore, he said, "You know what would have happened in the old days, if you had dropped me in the water?"

"Off with my head." John laughed, and then added, "But Your Highness, if you could walk on water, it would not have been a problem."

Kalakaua smiled. "I haven't learned that trick yet, but I will."

More long boats came ashore, until thirty men were assembled. "Mount up!" the king ordered. Men, horses, and wagons moved toward Kapaa, dust from the cavalcade smudging the air around them.

John leaped onto his horse and raced after the entourage, anxious about Kalakaua's safety, while at the same time curious to learn why the monarch had brought such a large party to Kauai.

An early morning shower coupled with a blazing sun had left the air sultry and humid. Beads of sweat formed on the king's brow and ran into his eyes. John offered him a kerchief and hat. "What brings you and your group to this island?"

Kalakaua shifted uncomfortably in his saddle. "The reciprocity treaty I made with America permits Hawaiian sugar to come into the United States duty free. It's like the gold in California. My club and I will build a sugar plantation in Kapaa and profit from this agreement."

John pulled at his straw hat, a feather lei entwined around its brim. He repositioned it to shade his eyes from the sun. He squinted at his friend, pausing before he spoke, knowing his words would be painful to hear. "You're paying a heavy price for being popular with the rich sugar folks. Most Hawaiians resent this treaty and the surrender of rights to Pearl River. People are saying that you sold out to the sugar plantations, getting nothing in return for Hawaiians."

When there was no response, John took a leap of courage and continued. "From what I can see, all you have done by this treaty is make people angry."

The king remained silent.

"Why do you think I'm here? It's to protect you from those who want to kill you for what you've done!"

Kalakaua wrung his hands, the bridle hanging loose on his saddle. "This was the peril four years ago: Lunalilo is dying. Foreign warships anticipating his death gathered in Honolulu harbor. Pro-American sentiment ran high in the white population. Rumors were flying that there would be a takeover if the anti-American Queen Emma was named our ruler."

John's eyes widened in disbelief. "Are you trying to tell me that you, a longtime opponent of annexation to America, decided to become king to save our independence?" He watched Kalakaua chew on a stick of salted scad and recalled how the sharp taste of the sun-dried fish bit into the tongue.

The king glanced around him, and then swallowed the morsel. "Whether anyone believes me or not, that is exactly what I'm saying. If Queen Emma had been selected to rule our kingdom, white businessmen would have supported an American takeover. My election saved our sovereignty."

John fixed his friend with an incredulous look and shook his head. "I suppose what you say is true, but Emma's supporters are angry. Some people are talking rebellion. The sugar planters are still taking our land for their plantations. They're even damming our rivers and streams and taking our water. And then they dare call us lazy and import foreign labor to replace us."

At this point, a rugged, weather-beaten man of medium size and build rode up to the king, reins in one hand and a corncob pipe in the other. Kalakaua said, "John, let me introduce Mr. Maxwell. He's going to be the labor contractor for my hui's new sugar mill in Kapaa. I leave you now, so that I can talk with others of my group." The king pulled his horse around and trotted away.

Maxwell extended his hand and John took it, finding the man's grip firm. "Good to meet you, Mr. Tana, the king has spoken glowingly of you. He says you saved his life awhile back."

John's eyes bore into the man, assessing whether his greeting was friendly or condescending. "The king makes too much of an incident with a crazy zealot. I was in the right place at the right time. Tell me, Mr. Maxwell, what do you think of the Hawaiian worker?"

After pulling deeply on his pipe Maxwell blew out a perfect ring. "The Hawaiian is as good a worker as you'll find. But like this smoke, they are disappearing. Yours is a dying race, Mr. Tana, and the plantations need the imported Chinese labor to build up the work force."

The answer surprised him. This was a factor John had not considered. Even if this were true, the immigration of laborers continued to puzzle him. "But why are plantation people bringing other races into Hawaii? Aren't the six thousand Chinese working in the sugar fields enough?"

Maxwell removed his pipe and leaned closer, their boots nearly touching. Lowering his voice, he confided, "Immigration of Chinese is going to stop. New people are being brought in to work, so we can keep the workers divided and control them. Avoiding labor unrest means more money for the planters."

Shaken by the ruthlessness of this plan, John asked, "With all this sugar money, are you going to build schools, roads, housing for the people?"

"That is for the Hawaiian government to provide, not the plantations. What Hawaii needs is a solid market economy and sugar will give us that." His pipe billowed sparks, he shook a finger. "In the past, Mr. Tana, your chiefs only cared about themselves. They had a golden product to trade in, sandalwood, but instead of husbanding the trees, reforesting as they cut, they denuded the hillsides, and gave away the sandalwood for very little in return. Your leaders were ruthless, they didn't care how many commoners they killed harvesting those trees. What did the chiefs do with the money? They spent it on frivolous things like silk and jade, leaving your kingdom with enormous debt, and wiping out the sandalwood forests along the way. Finally, there was nothing left to sell."

John felt chastised by the man's fervor and knew that what he said was true. "What about whaling, didn't that help?"

Maxwell relaxed in his saddle. Sunlight glinted through the leaves of a grove of coconut trees. Squinting at the men passing through the small forest he said, "Yes, whaling saved Hawaii for a time, but trading food to feed those whalers doesn't make money. It's the merchants with the smarts to buy and sell what the whalers need—ropes, sails, iron, all kinds of things other than food—that's how you make money."

John pulled at the brim of his hat and shook his head. "But isn't sugar food? I mean, you sell it, you're selling food. What's the difference between trading a pig and selling a pound of sugar?"

Maxwell sighed and gazed at John in a way that made him feel pitied. "Mr. Tana, it's simple economics. All over the world, people have pigs, chickens, and beef, but they don't have sugar. They demand sugar to sweeten what they eat. Sugar can be processed, packaged, shipped, and sold everywhere without spoiling. You can't do that with a pig. If Hawaii is to have a product to sell overseas, it needs sugar plantations. That means money brought to these islands. Over time, this wealth will trickle down to the common people and their lives will be better. The king is wise to make a reciprocity treaty with America. It is the foundation stone that will make everyone prosperous."

Chastised by Maxwell's remarks and struggling to grasp the lessons being taught, John mumbled, "I don't see that sugar plantations are benefitting Hawaiians. We lived well in the old days, when we could work as a family to grow what we needed and share with others."

"Patience, Mr. Tana, there will be opportunities for people like you. My advice is to buy land, the real source of wealth in Hawaii."

A cavalcade of riders passed the dunes of Waipouli, built high with the skeletons of marine animals tossed from the sea and blown into haphazard mounds by the winds. Grass and naupaka crowned the yellow-orange sand with fingers of green. Despite the softening of the shrubs, the beach reflected the heat of the sun, adding to the discomfort of the travelers.

Where the sandy coastline ended, it was replaced by jagged dark rocks thrusting beyond the fringing reef that protected the long shore. Giant waves smashed into the black lava rock, leaping high above the formations then falling with thunderous splashes, some of the water vaporizing on the hot stones.

The group ascended the low bluffs then moved upland, men fretting and stirring in their saddles, wearied by the hard travel. Red-yellow light rimmed the hills as the king's cavalcade drew up to a small village, its huts circling a large octagonal building. The king dismounted, and his courtiers entered the building to eat and be entertained.

John went to Kalakaua. "As I have said, Emma's people are rebellious. The sugar plantations have hired me to keep you safe. My men and I will patrol the area. Let me know when your party is ending."

Kalakaua laughed. "It may take all night."

"We'll be here." John saluted and signaled his two helpers, Kaipo and Kunani, to patrol the area while he reconnoitered the village. Boisterous voices accompanied by loud music jarred the night, and John could hear the visitors singing as they feasted, while partially-clad hula dancers swished around them. He was certain that the merry-making would last until midnight. Amber light flickered through the door of the party building as John probed the shadows of the village. The night turned cold and he shivered, drawing his coat more tightly around his chest. Despite his concern, it was peaceful, and he wondered if he was worrying too much. Deep in thought, he became suddenly aware that someone approached him.

"John, come with me," Kaipo whispered. He led him to a Chinese.

"Ayah, you Mr. Tana, friend of *pake,"* the man said, moving closer, as if wishing to confide something. "I throw away garbage, I see three men coming up hill, they talk. I hear them say they hide near horses, when they see king, they kill him."

"Kaipo, find Kunani. Tell him to stay with Kalakaua, no matter what, and to keep him inside. In ten minutes, meet me in the lean-to near the water trough."

Kaipo raced for the feasting hall. John moved with care, the only sound the soft crunch of his boots on the hard-packed dirt of the compound. His eyes scanned the darkness, seeking enemies. Nearly blind in the deep black of the night, he breathed shallowly, fearful of revealing his presence. He dropped to his knees by a hut and scanned the area around the tethered horses. He saw no one. He held his breath listening for sounds, but all he heard was the jingle of metal, the snorting of fretful animals, and the distant sounds of a raucous party.

Stars twinkled in a moonless night and blazing lantern light streamed from the open door of the octagonal building, illuminating the walkway that led to the horses. John scowled. *The king's enemies would easily see him when he walked from the party.* His heart hammered his chest. He inhaled slowly, the coolness of the late-night air easing the anxiety gnawing at him.

He sensed someone approach and he rose to a crouch, a knife drawn and ready. A shadow grew larger. He whispered, "Kaipo?"

A low grunt answered, his employee, bent low to the ground, shuffled into the shed. "See anything?"

"Nothing, but my eyes are still adjusting. Help me search."

The two men reconnoitered the area, but found nothing unusual. John worried that the Chinese was wrong, and any attack on the king might come from a different ambush point. *Should I fall back to the feasting hall and warn the king, setting up a line of protective bodies to save his friend from harm? But someone else could be hurt if the attack came while they defended him. "No,"* he thought. "*I must capture the assassins and learn how many others want the king dead.*"

He felt a hand on his shoulder. "Look at the trough," Kaipo whispered.

Cupping his hands, John studied the trough, straining to see what might be there. His eyes narrowed when he saw a lump and in the scarce light made out the outline of a head, then another, and another. "Good. We go around them. Take 'em from the rear."

Barely able to see, the two men crouched, then scurried from the low shed toward the water box. As John stepped closer he could hear men whisper, he strained his eyes to find them, learn of their weapons. His pulse pounded as he knew combat was imminent, but he stilled his breathing, his lua training kicked in and took control of his mind and body. A horse whinnied and the other animals moved restlessly, making jingling sounds as their reins clashed together. John motioned Kaipo to stop as he studied the shadowy figures. Had the horses sensed their approach? Surprise meant everything when you were outnumbered.

The hiding men fell silent and John saw one of them rise above the trough. He did not look behind, but crouched down muttering to his companions. John crept forward, motioning for Kaipo to follow.

Thirty feet from the ambushers, John loosened his tripping cord from his waist, holding its stones in his palm. He pointed with his head toward a man crouched at the edge of the trough. Kaipo nodded, loosening his nightstick from his belt, and moved toward him. John rose like a wraith springing from the earth, twirled the cord around his head, ran, and yelled, "Drop your weapons!"

Three men rose. One of them said, "Three against two? We're goin' give it to you." At that, the man reared back, a spear in his hand. John cast his tripping cord, the weighted rope snaked around the enemy body and John yanked hard, bringing his assailant to the ground, his spear falling at John's feet. A second man moved in, thrusting a knife.

John turned sideways. The blade slit his shirt making a shallow slash in his flesh. He gave the attacker a head butt and grabbed the hand holding the knife.

"I'll put your eyes out."

John shoved a knee into the man's groin. His assailant dropped his knife, clutched his loins, keening in pain. With his *piikoi*, John struck the man across the temple, bringing him down.

The attacker snared by the tripping cord staggered about trying to unwind the bindings. John came to him. "Surrender!" But the burly Hawaiian spat, swinging wildly with his fist. John blocked the awkward blow, shoved the ball of his piikoi into the man's belly, and smashed his forearm into his face. He went down.

Behind him, someone pleaded, "Let me go."

John wheeled and saw Kaipo with a man pinned to his side by an arm lock. "Hey, brother, you're bleeding."

John touched his sliced stomach, wet from a thin trickle of blood from his wound. "A shallow cut. Let's take these boys to the trough and cool them off."

The ambushers were dragged along the ground to the crib, their feet bound together. The two unconscious men were dunked into the water. John winced as he sought to revive them. He remembered Gonzalez and his use of salt water to sting his face and whipped back. Unlike the Portuguese, he had no intention of torturing the inert men.

When the two ambushers revived, John stepped back and said, "My name is John Tana, head of security at Princeville Plantation. Why are you trying to kill the king?"

When no one answered, he threatened, "We'll be here all night until you talk. If you do I will consider letting you go."

One of the captives appeared surprised. "You'll let us go if we tell you?"

"I'm not a liar, not a policeman. I'm only here to protect the king."

"My name is Kaleo," the man revealed. "These two are Manuela and Hiram. The three of us are loyal to Queen Emma, and we hate Kalakaua for selling out to the sugar people. Those plantation guys take our land, our water, they leave us nothing. Without work, we can't even feed our families, so we decided to get the guy."

John struggled with feelings of empathy for this man's plight. He knew that the Hawaiian was being squeezed by the thirst of the rich to seize land any way they could. *He remembered his own loss and the struggles he had undergone to survive in a new world that showed no pity for the ignorant poor. However, he had been asked by the rich to protect his friend, and assassination of the ruler was a capital offense.* John grimaced, his heart in turmoil with emotions. He shook his head. "I understand your pain, but killing Kalakaua is wrong."

"If you understand," the man called Hiram demanded, "then why do you help these sugar crooks?"

John chewed on his lip for a moment, again torn between his people's suffering and his obligation to protect the king. "We don't live in the old Hawaii, where the solution to problems was force and death. The coming of the foreigners has changed all that. Now we have laws that rule, and arguments are decided by courts, not combat."

"That is just haole bullshit," Hiram said.

"Whether you like it or not, you can't kill our king. He beat Emma in an election and she has accepted the decision of the voters. Kalakaua deserves a chance to do what he believes is best for his people."

The three men spoke as one, protesting that Kalakua was not their choice. It was rigged by the business guys. When John reminded them that an assassination attempt was an offense that called for hanging, the men fell quiet. "Lucky I stopped you before you did something stupid. What do you want to do? Hang, or go home and stay out of trouble?"

The three men talked quietly among themselves. Finally, Manuela spoke. "You have us in a tight spot. We hate the bastard, but we don't want to hang. Better to be a living resister than a dead man." The others nodded and promised to make no more trouble. John asked if there were other Hawaiians that felt the same. "Oh, yes."

"Tell them that they are not to harm the king. I'll keep your weapons. I'll be watching. If I see you anywhere near the king, or any harm comes to him, you will pay dearly for breaking your promise." With this, he untied his captives.

As they rushed off, Kaipo smiled. "You are a crazy man, but someone with a good heart."

"Find me a clean shirt," John said as the two men walked back to the party.

Kalakakua spoke to John the next day, "I'm told you let three assassins escape."

"No. They're on parole not to do you harm."

"You believe they will obey?"

"I have their word not to attack you."

"The only certainty is death."

"Do you think that hanging the three will help your popularity or make those who dislike you hate you more?"

The king paused for a moment then smiled. "So, you released these men making it appear I am benevolent."

"I don't know for sure, but three men swinging in the wind from a tree would either frighten or anger people. If you disagree then arrest me."

"Oh, ho, and make me more unpopular for punishing a man for having mercy on my enemies and saving my life? I will not do that. Instead, return with me to Honolulu. Emma has asked that I grant you the Royal Order of Kamehameha. I have my own award, the Knights Grand Cross. We will present them to you at a proper ceremony in the capitol."

"I'm not looking for awards."

"You will come. I command it."

Chapter 21

Honolulu

Thick smoke drifted over the green felt table top. Grant drew heavily on his cigar, studying the face cards showing in the game. "Are you going to bet, or just gape?" Jones said.

"Let's see how stalwart you are. I'll call and raise you ten," he said, throwing twenty dollars in silver on the table.

"That's more like it," Jones answered. "I call. Your turn, Kingsley."

Leinani's husband studied his cards, eyed his father-in-law, and smiled. "Kalakaua went to Kauai to open a new sugar mill in Kapaa. He's trying to cash in on the profits from the reciprocity treaty."

"Man got the treaty we wanted, but he doesn't know the first thing about growing and processing sugar cane," Jones scoffed.

"Yes, but James Maxwell does. He's with the king and his thirty court followers," Grant said.

"My information is that Maxwell is a sick man. Not long to live. Once he goes the king's enterprise will fail," Jones answered.

"That would be good for our interests. Kingsley, have you acquired the land surrounding the Kilauea River?" Grant asked.

"As you requested, I did."

"Good work. With our investments on the island and the Kilauea sugar mill in full operation we can monopolize production on Kauai."

"But we don't own the plantation," Kingsley said.

"Not yet, but my syndicate is buying up stock. We will soon control the company."

"But aren't you forgetting Princeville? The mill is still producing despite the fire that almost destroyed it," Jones said

"One more disaster, just one more, and Princeville is gone. My man Larsen knows how to create trouble, strikes, trashed fields, even fire—"

"With a man like your Swede, you don't need my Honolulu Rifles to help you," Jones said, then added, "Kingsley, are you going to bet?"

"I fold."

"Then it's my turn," Harold Summers said, the fourth man at the poker table. "By the way, have you seen the latest news? Kalakaua is going to decorate a Hawaiian with two Royal orders and make him a Knight of the Realm."

"That's positively medieval," Jones scoffed.

"Hardly, the giving of medals has become quite common in organized societies."

"Who is the lucky chap?" Kingsley asked.

"According to the paper his name is John Tana. Quite a story. Rescued two people stranded on the top of Waialeale and saved the king from assassins."

"Did you say John Tana!" Grant demanded in anger.

"Yes. Do you know the man?"

"He's a scoundrel. How can that buffoon king make awards without consulting us?"

"Are you going to make a formal protest to the king?"

"Not much good that will do. Gentlemen, my last hand. I must be about my business."

Once at home Grant looked for his wife. "That pesky kanaka has come back to bedevil us."

"Whomever are you talking about?"

"John Tana, the Hawaiian who burned my property and killed Gonzalez."

"I haven't heard that name in years. Wasn't your daughter in love with him?"

"Possibly, that is one of the reasons why I don't want him around meddling in our affairs."

"Have him arrested and thrown into prison. Can't you buy justice?"

"Kalakaua is going to make him a Knight of the Realm. He's a favorite of the king. My accusations will fall on deaf ears. There must be another way."

"Put Larsen and Gunter on the matter. I'm sure they can solve it for you."

"That will be the answer."

Chapter 22

John searched the dock for a familiar face as the *Kilauea* cruised into its berth. He didn't anticipate seeing someone he knew since he did not have time to message ahead his arrival from Kauai. But then he spotted a hulking brute of a man and called, "Aloha, Aaloa."

"Hey, you no-good Hawaiian. Where you been hiding?" the big stevedore answered. "What you up to?"

"Not much, got a date at the Government House."

"So, what you steal?"

"The island of Kauai."

The ship tied onto the wharf, a gangway descended, and John rushed off the boat. Aaloa grasped his friend and squeezed.

"Enough, big guy, let me breathe,"

"So, what's up?"

"The king wants to put some pins on my chest."

"When?"

"This afternoon at Aliiolani Hale."

"The Government House, that's a big deal. Can I come?"

"Put on a clean shirt, shoes and long pants. Be there by 3:00 today."

"So, I got to get pretty. For you I'll do it."

"It's not for me. It's for the party afterward."

"Can I bring some of the boys?"

"Sure, I think the king will love seeing his old militia pals."

"Yeah, too bad, once he got the top spot he had no more use for us. But he better watch out, them haoles are starting their own military."

"Maybe you can tell him tonight at the luau. I'm heading for Ah Sam and inviting him."

At the party afterward, John thought the ceremonies had been boring with too many dignitaries and long speeches. Others were honored, but he was the only person to receive two medals. At the event, he had searched the crowd for Leinani, but she was not there. *Just as well,* he thought. *She has a new life and I do not intend to interfere.*

Kalakaua drank champagne nonstop. When he decided to play *kilu* John knew it was time to go. He had no intention of playing the game where partners are swapped for sex so he asked the king for permission to leave.

"You don't want to try one of those hula girls? Too bad. Go if you must."

He searched for Aaloa and found the big man clutching two giggling women to his chest. John left, heading for Ah Sam's. His other friends were gone.

John picked his way along Merchant Street. Scant light from saloon businesses barely lit the road. He passed Alakea and sensed someone detach himself from a building behind him. Another man with a black hood over his face came at him with a club in his hand.

He instinctively dodged to the left, pirouetted on one foot, and drove the other into the hooded man's side. His opponent staggered. John swung his leg like a sickle and with a palm into the back, tripped him into the attacker coming from Alakea Street. Both fell onto the roadway. John followed up with a kick into the crotch of the hooded man, who howled in pain.

The second attacker rose from the street. He was almost as big as Aaloa and inches taller. John assumed a fighting stance. Feet square, fists closed at his sides, knees bent. He willed his body to relax and eliminate fear. He waited and watched.

The injured man attempted to rise, but groaned and fell back. His companion, also hooded, removed a long club from his side and began to sweep it as he slowly advanced. The whirling stick kept John from moving into him. He dodged left then right but the metronome-like movements of the heavy club thwarted any attempt to find an opening.

John feinted to the inside, but his opponent did not flinch and still swept his club. He realized that his enemy meant to drive him against a wall, then beat him to death. Only one option remained.

He turned and ran. The attacker yelled, "Coward," and started after him. John veered from Merchant onto Fort and found what he was looking for, a small stand of coco trees surrounded by a girdle of rocks. He pried out two stones and returned to Merchant.

His opponent hurried along the roadway. "Over here, asshole," John yelled, flinging a rock into him. The man gasped, lowering his club. John smashed the other rock into his jaw.

The hooded attacker's club brushed against John's shoulder. The blow stung, but did not bring John down. He smashed his rock into the side of his opponent's skull.

The man shook his head, dazed by the blow, but still had strength enough to sweep his arm into John's ribs, staggering him. The attacker's club swung down. John stepped to the side. The weapon smashed into the coral-surfaced street flinging shards of small rocks into the air.

Somewhere on Merchant Street a voice yelled, "What's going on?"

"Aaloa, help me."

The hooded attacker hissed, "I'll get you another time," and slunk away.

"What going on?" Aaloa asked.

John held his bruised side gasping to get air into his lungs. After several moments, he answered, "Two guys ambushed me. I got one of them down, but the other almost beat me. Did you pass anyone on the street?"

"No."

"Then they got away."

"Somebody wants to get you real bad."

"Yeah, and the only one in Honolulu who hates me enough to kill me is Robert Grant."

"That's a big shot haole. Don't want to mess with him. Talk to Kalakaua."

"He'll tell me it's my problem. I thought you were enjoying the party?"

"Saw you leave. I wanted to talk to you. Maybe you mention the militia to him."

"If I see him, I will."

"Walk with you to Ah Sam's?"

"I don't want them in danger. Could I stay with you tonight?"

"Sure thing, come on." The two men headed for King Street watching for any movements out of the shadows. Even with Aaloa by his side, John realized the big man he fought might beat them.

Chapter 23

Grant waved his cigar in a semi-circle around his office. Its tip glowed bright red from his fanning of the air. "Every time I send somebody to rid me of that kanaka, they come back defeated. What is it about that boy that turns grown men into flabs of jelly?"

"Not a boy. He's tough. My head still aches from the rock he hit me with," Larsen said, his tone surly.

"What about Gunter?"

"Stomach hurting, he'll be okay."

"Are you fit?"

"I can manage."

"It's time to finish him while he is in Honolulu. This is what we will do. Go to our Wailuku plantation, gather up six trusted supervisors, bring them to my warehouse on Queen Street."

"It'll take a couple of days."

"Do it today. Meet me tomorrow morning at the warehouse."

Larsen left.

Impatient, Grant paced the floor of his storage building. Mid-morning and no one had arrived. He reviewed the equipment on a table. There were several knives, clubs, nets, ropes, and two pistols. The noise of horses' hooves drew him to the main door. He pushed it open. Larsen and a half-dozen men dismounted and entered.

"I've asked you here to get this man," Grant said, distributing to each of his employees a newspaper with a picture of John Tana. "If any of you can capture him there will be a reward of one hundred silver dollars. He is dangerous. Arm yourself with any of these weapons." Grant gestured to the table.

"The pistols are reserved for Larsen and Gunter. If the occasion arises, kill him. There will be more money if you do."

"Police won't like us killing a Hawaiian," one man said.

Another added, "I didn't sign on as a *luna* to go hunting people."

"Then all I ask is find him and notify Larsen or Gunter."

"Do we get the reward if we spot him? How long we got?" several men asked.

Grant paused for a moment then said, "You'll look for three days. The hundred is paid only if you capture him. Otherwise I'll decide what your information is worth."

"Do we get paid while hunting?"

"Regular wages, Swede will give you your instructions. Find him."

Assignments were passed out and six plantation supervisors left. Grant spoke to Larsen, "Maybe you misjudged these boys' desire to help me."

"Best I could do on short notice."

"None of them are willing to take risks. How is Gunter?"

"He'll be ready. I think that the two I assigned to the waterfront want the hundred dollars. If they find him they'll capture him for you. Gunter and I say, if you want him dead we'll give him to you dead provided there's a bonus."

"There will be so long as you end the man's life without a trace. Maybe dump him at sea?"

Larsen nodded and left.

Chapter 24

John sat in the waiting room of the Government House. He went over the events of the previous two days trying to account for the threat to his life. "It's the publicity of receiving medals that caused Grant to attack," he muttered. Then he stopped himself from saying more for fear that others who waited might think him crazy. He felt that the longer he remained in Honolulu the more attacks would come.

"The king will see you now," a clerk interrupted his thoughts. He followed the functionary into an inner chamber. John was surprised at its opulence. Chairs of French design with edges of gold overlaying white painted wood furnished the room and a sumptuous desk of deep brown koa filled with papers and books where Kalakaua did his daily work.

The king smiled. "Brandy?" He poured a generous draft of liquor from a decanter on his desk.

"No, thank you."

"Well, I'll not waste good alcohol." The king downed the drink in a gulp. "What is it you want?"

"Members of the old militia want to see it brought back."

Kalakaua's eyes shifted away then returned to rest on his desk. "Hawaii no longer needs an armed force."

"But you were almost assassinated on Kauai and you needed to land American marines to stop riots when you became king."

Kalakaua's eyes shifted to the ceiling, "We don't need a militia. Whaling is a dead industry. Those sailors were the ones who caused trouble. We have a police force in Honolulu, that's enough. But I could use your help in another area."

"Ask and I will do it."

"Sad to say, but my sugar operations in Kapaa are failing. I need to close things up and bring my Hui Kawaihau back. Will you help my people to do this?"

"Yes."

John decided not to mention the attempt on his life. He felt certain Kalakaua would brush it aside as something to do with old enemies from the Chin Young murder case.

"Good. Are you prepared to leave? I have commissioned the schooner *Lady Jane* to bring my people back. It departs on the evening tide. It's at Pier Eight. I have a letter authorizing your passage and to work with my club. Of course, they know you as a friend but this will give your presence there added weight."

John took the letter and left, pleased with his good fortune to rid himself of Honolulu and danger. He went to the docks and had lunch with Aaloa. "Kalakaua won't bring back the militia. I think he doesn't want to upset the business community by having an armed force to call upon."

"Not the answer, brah. He no like spend the money. You saw the kind of parties he likes. Cost plenty."

John shrugged. "Maybe so, but a no is a no."

"One thing the guy don't understand, the haole that make him king can bring him down. They are getting ready. You watch."

"I hope you are wrong. I'll go to your place, get my gear, see Ah Sam, and say goodbye. I leave from Pier 8 on the evening tide."

"I see you there."

John saluted his friend and hurried off to Aaloa's home. He gathered his things, said goodbye to Aaloa's wife, and walked to Ah Sam's. At the doorway he helped build, he paused. On the street corner, a man with a white shirt, denim trousers, and straw hat stared at him. John stared back. The man dropped his eyes and shuffled away.

He pushed through the swinging doors. The savory aroma of sugared pig's feet made his mouth water. His Chinese friend saw him and motioned John to a table. "Lehua," he called. "Bring food for Uncle."

"No need, I come to say goodbye."

"Can't go without eating. Eh, take care of John."

Lehua brought a steaming plate of pork sausage, vegetables, sweet-sour chicken, and rice. A nagging feeling troubled John. *Was the man in the straw hat a spy*? He didn't want his friends to suffer again because of his enemies. Shaw was gone forever, but there was still Grant, and maybe that religious crazy man.

John took a few hasty bites then said, "Got to go. Shipping out to Kauai tonight. Just came to say goodbye."

"No leave so soon. Stay awhile. Children need to know their Uncle John."

Fear for Choi and Leinani jolted him. "Where are they?"

"At church school, I get them soon. Stay and say hello," Lehua said.

Worry creased John's face. He did not want his trouble visited on this family. "Lehua, Ah Sam, I have an assignment from the king. I can't stay. Kiss the children for me." With that, John grasped his friends, breathed their *ha*, and said goodbye. He hurried out the door.

After studying the street, he ran for the hills. When he was satisfied no one pursued him he returned to the harbor. The sun had set as he worked his way to Pier 8. In the deepening darkness, his innate caution caused him to use extra care to avoid being followed.

At Pier 8 a brown schooner lay tied to the dock. A few men loaded the ship and four men were on deck preparing for its departure. No one else stood near the boat. He stepped to the gangway and searched for the skipper. Spotting a man giving orders he called, "Sir, I have a letter from the king for passage to Kauai."

The officer signaled to come to him. He took the letter, read it, and said, "Right now I have no place for you to sleep below decks. You'll have to bunk on top. If I can sort things out, I'll try to give you better quarters. For now, store your gear over there." He pointed to the forecastle. "We leave with the tide, within the hour."

John thanked the skipper, stowed his gear, and returned to the dock, searching for Aaloa. Time passed, the loading had finished, and the crew prepared to cast off. He headed for the schooner, sorry that his friend had not come for some parting words. He reached the gangway.

"Eh, John, wait up," Aaloa called, stepping rapidly along the causeway toward the boat.

"How come you're late? Playing around with the girlfriends you met at the king's party?" John's face wreathed into a smile.

"Good thing I'm not like you, no like fun. I think you still a virgin," Aaloa answered, slapping John's shoulder with his palm.

"Eh, watch it. You almost knocked me in the water." The friends touched fists.

"Why you got to go so soon? You should stick around. We can party little bit."

"The king's sugar mill in Kapaa is finished. He wants me to help his group leave. I'm sent to pick them up and ship them here."

"So, Kalakaua's got you working for him? Gives you a couple of medals and figures you'll do what he wants."

"It's not that way. He's my friend."

"Your pal better watch his back. I hear lot of stuff. The foreigners not happy, they say he spend too much money on a good time. He's talking about going around the world. They'll get madder if he does. Big trouble coming for him."

"Mr. Tana," the skipper called. "Get on board."

"Well, good buddy, I hope you're wrong. Nothing I can do about it."

The two men embraced. Aaloa let John go and said, "You remember the first time we met? I called you 'sissy.' Look what we doing."

"Nothing wrong with good friends grabbing each other, so long as they don't break ribs, like you almost broke mine," John said, mimicking extreme pain.

"Eh, brah, if I want crush you, no can breathe for a month. Get on your boat." Aaloa waved John away as he stepped back into the shadows of a harbor building.

A seaman loosened a portside hawser at the front end of the schooner. John hurried onto the ship. Sailors raised the main staysail. He felt the tug of the wind and the pull of the tide on the vessel. The aft rope held the ship to the dock. A crew member worked to free it from the pier.

"Hold that ship," a man yelled.

The rope came loose from its fastening. "Jenkins, get on board," the skipper ordered. The sailor obeyed. The boat began to move from the pier, the rearmost hawser slowly slipping toward the sea.

Four men rushed to the stern of the schooner. One of them grasped the large rope pulling the ship back to the dock. Three of them jumped aboard.

"Get off my ship," the captain shouted.

"Not until we find that Hawaiian," a blond man said, drawing a pistol from his waist.

At the forecastle, John bent over his bag and retrieved his weapons, a club, sling, and choking cord. Two of the intruders stepped in his direction.

"Furl your canvas," the man with the pistol ordered.

"Lower the topsail," the captain shouted to crewmen hanging in the rigging.

The schooner slowed its movement from the pier.

John sheltered behind a pile of packing boxes. Breathing shallowly, he waited.

A bearded man appeared, a knife in one hand and a club in the other. His eyes shifted left and right. An instant before discovery John made his move.

His piikoi smashed the extended arm of his enemy. The knife clattered to the deck. The man swung a club. John stepped into the attacker's body, blocked his falling arm, and shoved the piikoi into his jaw. The man grunted and then howled as a knee went into his crotch. He collapsed to the deck grasping his lower groin as if his innards would spill out.

Before John could do more damage, a second assailant came at him, his knife jabbing. John retreated. The man assumed a crab-like stance, hunched over, knees bent, shoulders square, and arms pincers-wide, a weapon in each hand. He advanced like a scorpion, with his feet splayed out ready to move left, right, or straight ahead.

John backed into the portside rail. His opponent smiled. "Cornered, no place to go but into me." He made darting moves with his knife, short jabs that John barely escaped by twisting his body. Despite his efforts, the knife found its mark more than once. Blood dripped onto the foredeck.

John's back rubbed against shrouds pulled taut to the masthead. He reached up. His hands found a ratline. John bent his knees.

"Giving up, eh, it will not save you," his enemy taunted as he thrust his knife at John's chest.

John timed his movements, pulling himself up with his hands while springing with his feet. His lunging opponent passed under John's body. With his knees tucked into his chest John swung down, his buttocks smashing into the neck and back of his attacker.

The man fell onto the deck. John stomped his knife hand. The weapon clattered free. Instead of scrambling for it, his opponent rolled and got to his knees. John kicked at his face. The man leaned back. The blow glanced off his cheek, its force sufficient to unbalance him, and he fell.

By his side, John saw the bearded man upright, leaning against packing crates. "Get down, Abel," the blonde with the pistol yelled. John ducked. A bullet whined past his head. A club glanced from his shoulder and smashed into the portside rail. He tackled his opponent forcing him into the wale. The two men grappled.

"I can't get a clear shot. Let him go."

"I'm trying, but this kanaka got me pinned. Don't shoot."

John saw the gunman come forward from the rear mast, his pistol pointing in his direction. The schooner no longer moved. It bumped against the side of the dock. The sun had drifted below the horizon. It was dark, the moon had not risen. Faint light from the harbor was barely sufficient to outline the fighters. Against the starboard railing cowered several crewmen.

John kept Abel pinned to his body. The man fought to get free, flailing his club weakly against his back. Near the packing crates, the shooter tracked the fighters with his pistol. Its waver stopped. The trigger cocked.

A heavy rope whirred through the air striking the gunman. His weapon discharged into the deck. Aaloa whipped him again, and the pistol fell.

John head-butted his adversary and ran him like a battering ram into his other opponent who had risen from the deck. All three fell onto the planks in a tangle.

Miguel, a Grant supervisor, tried to interfere but Aaloa smashed his fist into his body. For a moment, they fought until the Bone Breaker picked him up like a sack and hurled him over the side.

A dazed Abel squirmed from the fight yelling, "Gunter, don't shoot."

The blonde gunman found his pistol. John grasped his hand. The two men wrestled along the deck. Gunter tried to force the weapon against John's head. With a massive effort, John squeezed the man's wrist, grasped the gun, and wrenched.

Bone broke. The pistol discharged. The ignited powder burned John's face. Its explosion deafened his ears. Gunter screamed. John wrested the weapon away from the Grant henchman and flung it into the sea. Aaloa stood near John, Abel grasped in a neck lock pinned to his side. In his other hand, he held onto the collar of the third supervisor.

"Thanks for the help. What happened to the guy on the dock?"

"He came charging on board to help. He is now swimming with the fishes. What you want do with these guys?"

"Gunter, you don't have a gun, your friends are finished. Who sent you?"

"I ain't talking."

"Aaloa, give your guy a little squeeze, maybe when he turns purple he'll say something."

"No more," Abel begged. "Let me go. I'll tell you what you want to know."

"Don't say nothing or you're out of job."

"Gunter, how well can you swim with one arm?"

"I can't swim."

"If you want to live, let the man talk, and if you fire him I'll come after you and make sure you're at the bottom of the sea. Okay, Abel, say what you know."

"I work at the Wailuku plantation with the other guys. Mr. Grant, the owner, promised a hundred dollars for your capture. I wasn't in on trying to kill you. That's Gunter's idea."

"You're the man who ambushed me after the king's party," John said, poking his finger into Gunter's chest. "Who was the big guy that worked with you? Another Grant employee?"

Silence.

John grasped the man's broken arm and twisted.

"Stop, please," Gunter begged. "The other man is Sven Larsen. We work for Grant."

"Where is he now?"

"I don't know. Looking for you I think."

Just then the captain interrupted, "We have to sail to make it to Kauai by nightfall tomorrow. If you have a complaint against these men, go ashore please, and see the sheriff."

John thought for some moments then said, "Gunter, tell your boss to stay out of my life. He can have my Kahului property. But if he keeps coming after me or my friends tell him I'll finish him forever. You and Abel can deliver the message."

Aaloa and the Grant employees left. The seamen pushed off from the pier, and the schooner headed for Kauai.

Chapter 25

Kauai, 1881

"Our mill is a failure," the king's steward complained. "Only rice can grow in this Kapaa marshland. Sugar cane rots."

John bit his tongue, refusing to say what he had known from the start of Kalakaua's enterprise. The king knew nothing of sugar cane growing, and neither did his court followers. Once Captain Maxwell died, the mill in Kapaa was doomed.

"You're selling?" John asked.

"Yes, the king's house in the hills, the land and buildings to Chinese rice farmers. The mill has been bought by Kealia plantation."

John did not answer. Instead, he bent to the task of helping Kalakaua's courtiers load possessions onto waiting wagons and dray them to long boats moored at the pier, then watched the boats move out to sea and unload onto the schooner anchored in a deep channel offshore.

After the last of Hui Kawaihau were on board the ship John left the black rock pier. He wondered whether he would ever return to the capitol. *Would Grant give up on his desire to see me dead? I gave the man what he wanted, my land. That should be enough.*

As he walked, he studied the town that had sprung up on a sliver of hardened earth bordering the extensive marshlands. *Only Chinese could find gold in the green algae swamps of Kapaa*, he thought. John knew that these former plantation workers, released from their labor contracts, had diked the swamps with iron tools, and loosened the rich mud with oxen-powered hand plows. *Damn, those pakes are smart. The only tool I ever had was a fire-hardened pointed stick.*

With a shrug, he mounted his horse, and turned toward home. He stopped when he saw the mountaintops to the north, covered with thick banks of cumulonimbus clouds that moved toward him in a stratospheric high wall. The immensity of this father of all storms blotted out the sunlight as it unrolled like a carpet over the island.

Gusts whipped John's body, forcing him to slip from the saddle and lead his horse forward. A mass of water dropped in huge twisting ropes, and the deluge slowed his travel. His horse whinnied, jerking at the halter. He held the tether tight, knowing that if the animal broke free and ran, he might never make it to Hanalei.

It took two days to reach the river. Sheets of rain turned the waterway into a raging torrent filled with broken trees and wood. Thunder blasted the valley, reverberating in sharp cracks that smote his chest, stifling his breath. Lightning flashed intermittently beyond the horizon, filling the grey sky with pulsing white light as jagged branches of electricity plunged into the sea. Water cascaded over the brim of John's straw hat blocking his vision, but he knew that he must cross the raging water and find his family. They were in danger. The floor of the valley lay submerged under the deluge.

Drops as big as fists splashed into his face, and John wiped his eyes, squinting at the raging torrent in search of the ferry that could take him across. Two barges laden with sugar cane stalks bounced and swirled in the river, the boatmen unable to control their crafts as the vessels raced for the sea. He tried to hail the men, but realized it was useless. His shouts were buried in the noise of the raging storm.

Hunger gnawed his belly. He had only chewed on stalks of dried fish during his journey. He wished for a hot meal, but realized it would be a long time before he ate warm food again. He worried about his family and he hoped that they were safe and not starving as he was. *At least there is plenty of water*, he thought as he pulled his skittish horse along the river searching for the ferry station.

It was not long before he came upon three men and their horses standing by a passenger scow tethered to the eastern bank. Earth-colored water smashed into the side of the vessel, rolled around the ends and then rushed on.

A Chinese stood on its wooden platform clutching the traversing rope, arguing the dangers with the men. He shook his head many times while pointing to the turbulent water. When he spied John, he beamed, "If you help me, I will go."

John nodded.

The Chinese instructed his passengers to enter the craft and stand on the opposite side of the current. The horses proved a challenge. It took forceful pulling to get them onto the barge. When the ferryman felt satisfied with the loading process, he asked John to seize the traversing rope and, with him, pull the scow across the river.

"One, two, three, heave!" the boatman yelled. The ferry moved from its safe mooring into the raging river. "One, two, three, heave!" Water stormed against the side of the scow, cascading over it, flooding its floor, and then sweeping out though the sloping entryways. Strong currents heeled the scow, causing the ferryman to slip on its floorboards and fall into the turbulent water.

John let go of the rope, leaned, and seized a flailing hand of the drowning man. He pulled him from the river, rolled the Chinese toward the passengers huddled along the far railing, and yelled, "Hold onto him." He returned to the traversing rope and heaved, forcing the stubby vessel through the crashing torrents. Its tilt increased as the scow planed over the roiling waters, the men on the far railing ankle deep in water cascading over the wooden edge of the boat. John pulled once more, the power of his thrust speeding the flat-bottomed craft into the tall grasses growing along the western bank.

With everyone ashore, John rode toward Sui Young's compound. Shrieking wind whipped rain into him. His horse stumbled. The animal made crying sounds as stinging darts of water blasted his body. John draped his slicker over the animal's head, hoping to lessen its fear. To the left, rice fields were little more than drowned tips of leaves peeping above a sea of water.

Squalls beat into John as he rode into the compound. He dismounted, his legs sinking into swirling water that rose to his knees. The walls of the settlement were underwater, and Chinese men rushed about, loading wagons whose wheels were partially hidden by the flood. He saw Sui working among them and yelled over the wind, "Have you seen my family?"

Sui shuddered then yelled back, "No. Maybe Hawaiians go to the mission. If rain doesn't stop, whole valley, even mission will be ocean. We set up camp on hill over there." He pointed to the southwest. "Find family, bring them, be safe with us."

John nodded. He thought to ask Sui for food, but rejected it. He could not wait. He mounted and urged his horse through the deepening water. Rolls of thunder rumbled like gunfire through the valley. The horse shinnied so violently that John dismounted to get it under control. He led it the final stretch into the Hawaiian village where waves washed against the horse's belly. All around him, shacks and buildings were submerged. Objects bobbed on the surface, while chickens, hogs, and domestic animals clung fast to anything that was anchored or floated. The only ones that seemed unfazed were the ducks, who paddled about, quacking and dipping for food.

John waded to his home. He called. No answer, the building stood empty. He realized that if anyone still lived they must have sought refuge at the mission. He pulled his tired horse away from the deserted village and toward Waioli Church. In the gloom, he made out its spire and forced his way through the water, his body aching with the struggle.

As if in a trance, he staggered to the steps of the mission. The flooding water had not yet reached it. A frightened Hawaiian woman stood at the top of the stairs. He asked for his family. He heard a noise behind her, and then a keening cry as Mahealani rushed to him, oblivious of the rain. At that moment, worry and tension were released. He mustered his energy, charged up the steps and enfolded her into his arms. "You're safe, you're safe," they both murmured. John kissed Mahealani on her face, her hair, pressing her to him, his heart filled with relief. She, in turn, clung to him, returning his kisses, her eyes shining with joy, their words of love lost in the wind.

John pulled himself away. "Where are the children?"

Mahealani took John by the hand and led him into the church. Standing inside was his daughter clutching JJ's hand.

With a whoop and a shout that echoed through the building, John rushed to them, gathered them close and hugged them to his body. "I love you so much, forgive me for leaving you."

The water that covered the mission grounds insinuated its way into the church. In the distance at the southwest end of Hanalei Valley, and on a plateau sixty-feet high, John saw the little community of temporary shelters built by Sui Young and Li Lao Tse.

With his family and several stranded Hawaiians, John rowed a longboat to the camp. When they were close, he hailed the Chinese. Familiar faces peered over the plateau's edge. The boat bobbed dangerously in the eddying waters. Li Lao Tse yelled for them to catch a rope he threw. As soon as the rope was secure, all the castaways but John and a second man, Kamalani, climbed to safety.

"Take care of them!" John called to Lao and Sui Young. "I'm going back." His friends waved their acknowledgement. John and his companion detached the rope and oared to the mission. The storm continued to rage and the wind howled, whipping the water into cresting waves that smashed into the boat, rocking the vessel like a baby's crib.

As he neared the church, John saw a shivering Chinese standing on the porch. The water had risen to the same level as the top step. John's boat bumped against submerged wood to the point where the man stood. The Chinese was close to panic.

John calmed him enough to learn his name was Chang. With a wavering voice he said, "Mud come down on homes of Princeville supervisors. All buried, come help."

Chapter 26

With Chang as their guide, John and Kamalani pushed away from the church, oaring into murky waters filled with torn bushes, broken trees, wrecked buildings, and dead animals. The debris whirled and swung about, moving mindlessly with the vagaries of the currents. John's thoughts drifted to Noah, and he wondered if the deluge would submerge the whole island. Beneath the boat ocean fish darted, startled by the splashing oars. It struck John that if this rain continued, the only survivors of the deluge would be these fish, but then he saw mouths gasping above the roiling surface of the water and he realized that above this brackish flood the sea fish searched for oxygen to survive. He shuddered. *If the island sinks beneath the waves then I and those I love could be gasping for air like those fish.*

His muscles knotted as he returned to the oars, seeking to wash away his gloomy thoughts with the strain of rowing. He was bone tired after three days with little sleep, but he willed himself to go on. He had worked at the plantation for several years, and knew some of the supervisors. Though they did not mix with the Hawaiians, and even despised them, he felt a loyalty to the company, and would do what needed to be done.

He looked at Chang standing at the prow. "Are we near the mill?"

The Chinese peered into the unnatural darkness.

"We should be near the river by now and feel its swift flow."

Chang shook his head.

John put his hand into the water. He did not sense strong currents pushing the vessel to the sea, and he wondered if they were traveling in circles.

"Ayah," Chang shouted, "there is pier." John followed the man's pointing and saw the wooden platform of the dock barely visible under a layer of water. He was surprised by its nearness, and realized that the entire valley was submerged beneath the sea, and water was washing inland instead of washing out. The boat bumped against the dock. The three men jumped out, pulling their vessel until they found a patch of mud to hold the boat.

John stared at the hillside above the mill, wondering if the heavy rain had softened the soil enough to cause another avalanche. Chang busied himself searching for help, and found several workers huddled beneath a makeshift shelter on high ground. He yelled at them seeking information, and discovered that a crew of Chinese was at the earth slide.

"You have boat, we come with you to help," one of the men said. Shovels and picks were collected and they set off. Guided by hau trees thrusting above the submerged riverbank the rescuers rowed against the light current. John was alarmed by the rising water, worried that the homes of the supervisors had been shoved under it.

Soon the men saw a collapsed hillside splaying out in a mountain of dirt. A tiled roof and part of a house stood visible in the rain. Nearby a second home buttoned into the landslide, water swirling around the broken building, turning loose earth into mud, darkening the river a deep brown.

John steered the rowboat into the muck as his men leaped out into the dirt with shovels and picks, digging away the loose earth around the first house. John searched for an entry, anything to get into the building. Within moments he found a smashed window, and with Kamalani's help squirmed inside.

Wet dirt covered the floor of the living room. The two men slipped in the ooze, slithering through the mud as they struggled to find their way in the dim light. The house creaked, tilting slightly, and John's feet lost traction, slipping into the wet dirt. Against the far wall a mound of earth had burst into the building, a head and hand visible in it. Sliding to the buried man, John yelled to Kamalani for help as he dug with his fingers, fearful that an iron tool might cause injury. A Chinese came through the window and helped clear mud from the trapped man. The house creaked and slid. Water crept into the room turning the earth into a pond of brown paste, from the broken wall more dirt flowed in.

John fought panic as he saw that the ooze would soon smother the trapped man, and endanger the rescuers. "Kamalani, you and the others dig this guy out. I'll force my body into this mush and dam it before the man's head becomes submerged."

"But this loose stuff could bury you," Kamalani yelled.

"Do it," John said as he fought into the muck pushing his body against the trapped supervisor, protecting his head and face from the slime. The rest of his men tore at the loose earth freeing the man from the sludge. As they pulled him away, the mound collapsed in a small avalanche, partially burying John.

Kamalani seized his arm. John floundered in the dirt, seeking traction. Helped by the Hawaiian, John came free of the sucking ooze and yelled, "Get outside before this house slides into the river."

"June," the supervisor mumbled.

"Where?"

"River…" the man said, lapsing into unconsciousness.

John yelled over a rising wind, "You men search as best you can. Try to get into the other home. See if anyone is in it. I'm going in the rowboat to look for June."

As he worked the oars, John thought it was a hopeless task to find a woman in the gigantic bowl of water that Hanalei had become. But though he despaired, he shouted, "June, where are you?" He hollered his message several times, but the only sound was the patter of rain.

With an uncanny suddenness, the wind died and the deluge from the sky reduced to a drizzle. A weak light peeked through the canopy of clouds. John crisscrossed what was once the river, continuing to call, "June". The current was light and easily managed, and he made swift progress through the water, searching along the bank for a human form. He worried that the increasing darkness would force him to end his search.

The daylight turned grey and still John hollered, "June." He paused, letting the boat drift with the current, listening for an answer from a far-off voice. There was nothing but the murmur of rushing water and the sounds of dripping raindrops sliding down leaves into the lake.

"June," he called, his voice knifing through the eerily still air.

No answer came, but John thought he saw cloth. A boat-length away, an uprooted tree lay mired in the river with strips of a garment trapped in its branches. He rowed to it, searching. He spied more cloth, then a head, and part of a woman's body wedged into the twigs. He rowed to her, but was unable to push the boat through the tangle of limbs.

Flinging a rope onto the tree, John entered the water, swimming against the gentle current. He pushed his body into the branches, their sharp points pricking his skin, tearing his flesh. He reached the woman, trapped in a web of broken twigs. He tried to free her, but waves of water cascaded over his head, blinding him. He dove into the murk, feeling around her body, breaking the slivers of wood that pierced June's clothing, twigs that saved her from drowning, but now were holding her trapped to the tree.

John felt her move with the current. He cupped a hand under June's chin and eased her from the branches, her clothing shredding in pieces. When her body slid into his, John felt its coldness. He wondered if she still lived.

Lifting the nearly nude woman into the boat was difficult, but John put his hands under her arms and pulled her in. He held her close to listen if she breathed. Her water-soaked hair draped over his shoulder, a cheek touched his, and a faint warm breath flowed over his face. For a moment, the woman's nudity, her tormenting words at the beach party, stirred him. The boat spun from the tree and into the heart of the river. Shaking away his thoughts, John lowered June onto the floor of the craft, seized the oars, and rowed toward the mudslide.

Chapter 27

Waterfalls and Hanalei Fields

Three weeks later, the afternoon sun glowed crimson over Waialeale, warming the valley of Hanalei. Clouds floated above the dead volcano. From the mountain, water fell thousands of feet in broad, white, sheets into pools of green water. Rainbows filled the valley with crescents of color. Harry Low, Princeville Plantation's current manager, sat with John Tana, the men gazing at nature's beauty from the veranda of Low's home. "Mesmerizing, isn't it? Flowers are blooming, trees thrusting out new leaves, everything is growing. Yet just a few days ago, the greatest flood in history hit Hanalei Valley, burying everything under fifteen feet of water."

"I understand you lost a thousand acres of sugar cane, rotted by the flood."

"Yes, plus severe damage to the mill and warehouses. I don't think the plantation can recover."

"Are you telling me that you might be finished, that I might be out of a job?"

Low squirmed. "I can't say with certainty that our sugar days in Hanalei are over, but our debts are huge, the damage is great, and I see little chance of recovery. Then there is the problem that we can't get water from the Kilauea River to feed our upland acreage."

When John said nothing, he added, "I'm grateful that you saved my assistant manager's life, and that of his wife. They've taken a leave of absence and are in Honolulu for medical care. Before they left, they wanted me to convey their appreciation." Low smiled, as if guarding a secret. "Oh, and June said you are handsome, strong, and very intelligent, and that she didn't know that Lothario was a friend of Don Quixote."

John laughed, recalling the moments with her on the beach at Kalihiwai. Her softness as she lay limp against his body. "Mr. Tucker has a very smart wife. I am relieved that I could answer her question."

Low stared at John for a moment. "I think you should find another security position. I've spoken to the manager of Kilauea Plantation and I told him of your splendid work. He's interested in speaking with you."

John shook hands with the manager. "Thank you for everything." Mounting, John gave a smart salute, turned the horse away, and galloped along the plantation road leading into Hanalei Valley, a refreshing wind from the sea blowing against his back.

Warm shades of red, orange, pink, gold, and yellow flamed over the high cliffs of Na Pali. A veil of dark blue shadow covered the shield wall of Waialeale Mountain as the rays of the descending sun were deflected by the height of the dead volcano.

Chapter 28

Honolulu

"Robert, a delightful Scotch, best I have ever had." Donald Cartwright sat in a plush red chair in Honolulu's Downtown Club. He tossed down his drink and walked over to the sidebar and a decanter of Scotch, its rich alcohol gleaming golden orange.

"I'm glad you enjoy it. I'm importing the finest liquor money can buy. Sugar profits have gone through the roof since the reciprocity treaty with America. I can afford the best for my friends."

Grant frowned as he passed a plate of cured beef to Bruce Jones. "Yet there is a nagging problem, the labor situation. Those damn Chinese are scoundrels. Not re-signing labor contracts, and those that do are making demands for better working conditions, more money. They stir up the new importees to strike."

Cartwright refilled his glass. Waving it at Grant he said, "What do you propose to do? The Chinese dominate our work force. What about the Hawaiians?"

"Hawaiians! They are worthless. We can't force them to work as hard as the Chinese, they claim too many rights, and unlike the pake, our courts give them protection. It's better to take their land while they are still ignorant and immersed in the past. I propose we bring in more foreign laborers from other countries. A boatload of Portuguese came in a while ago. Good workers. No trouble. We can import Germans, Norwegians, Fijians, Japanese, and other races. Dilute the work force. No one group a majority. We end our reliance on China for cheap labor. Then we squeeze the Chinese who are here," Grant said, taking a long pull on his cigar, its tip glowing red as he drew in smoke. He hissed it out in a spiraling grey cloud.

The door to the private room opened, and Grant's son-in-law entered. "Kingsley, good you could come." Grant smiled a welcome. "What's the news on Princeville Plantation?"

"I think they are on the verge of collapse. That move to acquire the land along the Kalihiwai and Kilauea rivers was brilliant. Then your refusal to allow Princeville to take water has ended any chance they might have to grow sugar cane in the uplands. Following your instructions, I have foreclosed on their equipment and it is only a matter of days before they fold."

"Capital, and you have financed the new tools for Kilauea, the railroad, steam plows, centrifugal separators?"

"Yes, all has been done as you requested. I believe with plenty of water and new equipment. Kilauea will become a powerhouse plantation."

"Good. I am buying up land on the north shore of Kauai. You men should do the same. If anyone stands in our way, we will squash him."

"What about our king?" Cartwright asked.

"For now, he is a minor inconvenience," Grant answered. "He drinks fine champagne, enjoys the hula, and women too."

"But he could be trouble in the future. He's Hawaiian and has revived cultural practices long dormant, like belief in the kahuna. He could send a ghost to bedevil us." Cartwright laughed.

"Rumor has it he is considering a world tour," Kingsley said. "He is heading to Japan first."

"Good, let him be away for a while. We can grow our profits while he's gone." Cartwright rubbed his hands together. "And we need Japanese workers to counter Chinese trouble makers. The king can make some deals to import them."

"Enough talk about Kalakaua. We have sugar mills sprouting up all over these islands, and if you men listened to my conversation with Kingsley you would have heard about steam. The day of the oxen is over. A team of animals can only haul three miles in a day. The radius between mill and fields can only be that distance. Track laying can be done almost anywhere and the hauling distance is unlimited."

"And the steam plow is a wonder machine," Kingsley interrupted. "Eighteen oxen can plow a furrow of earth two miles in an hour. Two steam plows can dig up three grooves in a field three times that distance in the same time."

"Astounding," Cartwright said.

"And that is not all, new mill equipment can process cane into sugar faster than ever," Grant added. "So long as we keep wages at rock bottom, our sugar earnings will soar."

"You think that bringing in races other than Chinese will do that for us?" Jones asked.

"Yes, divide and rule, and steam, that is the way to lower our costs."

Cartwright came over with the bottle of Scotch and a tray of four glasses. He poured the alcohol and said, "Gentlemen: a toast to profits."

Chapter 29

Kauai

Kilauea Plantation's manager, Charles Gordon, scoffed at the notion that security might be needed. "We haven't had trouble. No reason to seek help."

John, dressed in long black pants, white shirt and uncomfortable dark shoes, answered humbly, "Mr. Low thought you might need assistance. You have Hawaiian workers. You're bringing in more Chinese. I hear there may be Fijians, Portuguese, and other races who will be brought in to work your land. There could be friction between them. Princeville suffered a serious fire that hurt them, that's why I was hired. Once on duty no further trouble occurred."

"Let me think on it. Low gave a glowing recommendation. He also mentioned your security work in Hanalei and your friendship with the king. I'll talk to my partners and let you know. Where can you be reached?"

"Waioli Mission."

John left the manager's office discouraged that he would not get a new job. Security work in Hanalei was an easy chore, the Chinese respected him and often came to him for advice when trouble brewed. But he was concerned for the helpers he had hired once he lost the Princeville job. Without it there would not be enough wages to pay the two men and keep his wife happy.

When he arrived at home, Mahealani asked, "Did you get it?"

John shrugged. "He put me off. 'Think about it.' With no new job, it will be difficult to pay for Kaipo and Kunani and stay here in Hanalei."

"No worry. We will manage. Even go back to Anini Beach."

John could see disappointment edged in her face. Nani and JJ had started school at the Mission. Mahealani attended classes to educate herself. He knew she would accept any decision he made to share what they earned from rice profits. "To make us happy we need a party. Invite Al, your family, our friends."

Mahealani clapped her hands. "I'll get things ready. You get a pig and we will roast it in the imu. No alcohol, mission people believe it makes Hawaiians crazy. Send Kaipo, Kunani over the hill to invite Akaka's family and mine. We have fun tomorrow night."

Next evening, friends from Kalihiwai joined the family for the luau at John's Hanalei shack. Mats were spread out beneath a tall hala tree. On it were platters of poi, raw fish, limpets, roasted pig, stewed chicken, fruits, and coconut dessert.

The Alapai family had sent word that they could not come. Mahealani worried over their refusal. "Talk to Al, find out why."

As guests gorged themselves on food, John approached Akaka. "Having a good time?"

"Everything is first class."

"I've been watching you. You seem to want to tell me something, but have kept things bottled up. Why?"

A troubled look spread over Akaka's face. "I didn't want to spoil your party with the news from Anini." He paused for a moment and then, in a confidential tone, said, "Things are in turmoil. You need to see Haku. Your mother-in-law is sick, weak. She fears falling asleep. Anuhai speaks of something coming in the night, turning her feet cold. Whatever it is has spread into her stomach."

Chapter 30

John left early for Anini Beach. His thoughts were troubled. He had not told Mahealani the reason for his journey. Their disputes over the old religion had died. She appeared to have accepted Christianity, even sang with the mission choir. But he suspected that deep inside, his wife harbored fear of the kahuna. *In my heart*, I *know our conflicting beliefs could tear our marriage apart.*

The day was bright. The ocean sparkled. Gentle waves washed over the fringing reef and lapped onto the sandy shore. It was peaceful. John thought, *there could not be evil spirits haunting this special place.* When he rode into the Alapai compound, he saw Haku sitting outside his home, stripped to the waist, mending a throwing net. When the old man spied John he scowled, his eyes wary.

Haku stood, his forehead furrowed as he greeted his son-in-law and asked after Mahealani and the children. Satisfied with the answers, Haku demanded, "Why are you here?"

John frowned. Haku acted defensive, maybe fearful of wrongdoing. John knew that Anuhai had recently accepted Christianity, but Haku refused conversion. *Had he turned to the kahuna for help instead of the Christian God*? Despite the danger of re-kindling their differences over paganism, John bluntly said, "I came because of Anuhai. Akaka told me that she's sick."

Haku smoothed his palm over the stubby white hair on his skull, stroked his grey beard. He leaned closer and in a conspiratorial tone, as if Jesus might hear, he whispered, "I know you don't believe in this stuff, but Anuhai claims an uhane has entered her body. It is coiling and uncoiling within her stomach."

A creaking sound came from behind them. John gave a start, then saw it was an Alapai youngster opening the door of the house that he had helped finance and build for the family. He pursed his lips, grasped the older man's shoulder. "What medicine are you giving her?"

Haku shrugged off John's hand, a look of defiance in his eyes. "I called in a kahuna. She claims an evil spirit possesses Anuhai. So far, her efforts have not worked. My wife is dying. The kahuna is asking that the family come to confess sins as a last resort to save her. I'm sending for the family to gather here."

"This is crazy. I have told you, the kahuna's black magic does not work. I'm going to see her." With that, he stepped into the home and knocked at Anuhai's door. A thin woman with a skirt of ti leaves bound tight around her waist, opened it. Her hair hung in strings around her face, draping over her shoulders in thin strands of black and white. Her chest was bare. Her breasts sagged like lumpy bags onto her belly. She was toothless and mouthed some words through thin lips that John could barely understand.

Anuhai lay still on the sheets, covered by a tapa, with her head propped against several pillows. Her eyes fluttered open. She saw John and said, "I'm happy you came."

They exchanged breath and John asked, "What's wrong?"

"Uhane in body," the creature behind him screeched.

He saw Anuhai shaking her head. John turned to the old woman and pointed to the door. As she slowly walked away, John heard her muttering incomprehensible words. John returned to the bedside. He kissed Anuhai's brow, felt its coldness, and knew his mother-in-law was sick.

Anuhai whispered, "After you saved me from the octopus, I've been very careful. Maybe someone's angry with me." She took a moment to catch her breath before adding, "I don't go fishing, and I take my hair, fingernails, even my uneaten food, and I bury them." Having spent all her energy, the old woman fell back onto the pillows and closed her eyes.

John stroked her hair, rubbed her back. She woke as if she suddenly remembered something. She grasped his hand. "A week ago, I fell asleep in the woods. Near the old *ahupuaa*. When I woke, some of my hair had been cut.

I thought I heard a voice saying, ‘Uhane will come’. Three days later, by this house, there lay a bag of ape leaves wrapped around my hair. Every night since then, a ghost comes in my dreams.”

Haku Alapai stormed into the room. “The kahuna tells me you sent her away. You’re not practicing your Christian beliefs in this house.”

“No, I am not. Is the woman ana ana?”

“Not a death dealer. A *kahuna lapa au*, a healer. She claims the family has offended someone. A mighty kahuna has sent an uhane to possess and kill Anuhai. The family will come together. Confess sins. The kahuna will listen and decide the cure.”

Unable to restrain himself, John said in a terse voice, “Belief in the kahuna is wrong. Anuhai is sick, but not by an evil spirit.”

Haku’s face became hard. He looked John in the eye and said, “An uhane infects Anuhai. Only the kahuna can save her.”

John stopped his protests. He knew it to be useless. He thought he would speak with Mahealani and see if she could convince Haku to relent. Yet he felt a nagging worry that she believed as her father did.

“The family will come together as the kahuna demands. Send word to Hanalei for my daughter and her children to return!” Haku ordered.

Chapter 31

Once the family gathered, the kahuna said, "Anuhai is going to die. Someone has offended a powerful person. We must find out who it is. Each of you will confess your sins to others. Then I find a way to save her."

John whispered to Mahealani, "This is black magic foolishness. Your cousin had coldness in his stomach. Your family tried to save him by making offerings to the kahuna. He died. We are Christians and should not believe in this kind of superstition."

"My father is right to do this. We will do what he wants."

John ended further argument. He realized that despite being Christian, Mahealani still believed in sorcery. He would wait and find a chance to challenge the falsehood of the old religion. As he listened to the confessions John realized that family members were like him, reluctant to admit to wrongdoing. When it was her turn, Mahealani looked at him and simply said, "I have offended no one except my husband and he would not hurt my mother."

Anuhai was the last to make her confession. As the kahuna begged for silence, John wondered why the victim of the uhane had not been the first to speak. But then he decided that forcing everyone to share their guilt first asserted the kahuna's power over the family. The hag uttered a short prayer to the gods, then asked Anuhai to confess.

"Maybe three years ago, I was gathering ti leaves in the hills. I thought I heard a human sound. I ignored it, for I believed it was goats feeding in the hills. The voice came again. I looked and saw..." Anuhai faltered, her hands went to her belly, kneading it.

Haku moved toward his wife, but the kahuna restrained him. "What did you see?" she demanded.

Anuhai gathered herself. "I saw a scrawny old man among the trees. He was naked. He beckoned me to come to him. I ran away."

"Was this before the octopus attack?" John interjected.

The kahuna scowled. "Silence," she commanded.

Anuhai nodded.

Haku began to bluster, but a withering look from the old witch stilled his tongue. The kahuna glared at John, then returned her stare to the sick woman.

The witch's baleful look prompted Anuhai to continue. "At a luau in Kalihiwai not long ago, an old man took an interest in me. His name was Hawae."

The kahuna hissed, sucking in her breath.

Flustered, Anuhai stopped, but continued when the sorceress demanded that she reveal everything that happened at the party. "Hawae followed me everywhere. He was the same man who wanted me years ago."

The old woman wept, covering her face. In the momentary silence, John looked at Mahealani, wondering what had been the price for the love potion she received in the past. He had never learned the truth. His glance shifted to Haku and he could see that his father-in-law wanted to speak.

"Haku was not at the party," Anuhai continued. "The old man cornered me in the darkness. He demanded love. I knew sex with him would be horrid and at first, I said nothing, hoping by my silence he would go away. But he asked again, grasping for my breasts. His breath smelled of alcohol. It was terrible." The woman paused, her body trembling.

After she controlled her shaking, she continued, "I pulled away from him saying, 'You are an ugly drunk. Never will I sleep with you.' To escape, I hit him and ran home."

"You never told me this," Haku said, anger in his voice.

"What would you have done?" Anuhai answered, her voice weak, her tone scornful. "Fight the ana ana? No, you would have done nothing!" She rose from her pillows, spitting out the words. Haku hung his head, acknowledging the truth of what she said.

A babble of voices erupted. Alapai family members spoke of seeing an old man in the woods near the compound and on the hills overlooking the fishing grounds of the beach. John approached the witch woman, who was muttering by Anuhai's side, and asked, "Who is Hawae?"

The scrawny kahuna's hands fingered her face. She placed her chin on her fists and in a reedy voice said, "He is a powerful death dealer. Expert in poisons: lau hue, kukui, ape juice. It will take many sacrifices and gifts to counter his evil plan."

John did not believe the shaman. He knew she would take what she could from the Alapai family, and let Anuhai die without medical help. He expressed his doubts to Mahealani who wailed, "Evil will come to us if you reject the kahuna. The Christian God cannot save my mother, only the kahuna woman can."

Believing that there was a more rational explanation for Anuhai's illness, John sought out Haku Alapai who was shaken by his wife's confession. Already the old witch had made demands upon him that Haku was unable to fulfill.

"Is there a favorite beverage or food that only Anuhai eats or drinks?" John asked.

The older man rubbed his bulging stomach, big as a barrel of whale oil, and said, "In the woods near the ahupuaa there's a still where mama makes beer for herself. It's hidden from the police."

John retrieved the ape leaves that had been wrapped around Anuhai's hair and asked Haku to show him the still. The two men walked into the woods. Memories of the death of his lua teacher troubled John's thoughts and he trudged in silence. He had not drunk alcohol since that tragedy. When they came to the still, John tasted the brewed beer. Rinsing his mouth, he bit into an ape leaf. He spat out what he chewed. He said to Haku, "The beer is poisoned. It has the taste of ape juice. If Anuhai stops drinking this brew she'll get well."

It took much discussion and taste testing before Haku agreed to the advice. John smashed the still, but not before he filled a gourd with its adulterated alcohol. At the family compound, he spoke with Mahealani, "I am going to Kalihiwai to see Akaka. Together we will find this Hawae and end his poisoning of your mother."

"John, Hawae is very powerful. He is a great kahuna. He can send one of his many souls into an animal and make it do his bidding. I'm sure he is the one that conjured up the ghost that frightened our son. Leave him alone."

"I don't understand how you can say that. We are Christians. You must not believe in black magic."

"I am afraid for our family. Leave Hawae alone. The still is broken, that is enough."

Troubled by her pleading, yet determined to end the hold that the old beliefs had on his wife and the Alapai family, John left for Kalihiwai.

That evening he met with Akaka, asking him about Hawae and where he lived.

"He is a creepy guy. Claims he can pray people to death. I don't believe that, but I don't want any trouble, so I'm friendly with him. Hawae lives far up the river near the base of the mountains. Spend the night with me and tomorrow we will search for him."

Chapter 32

A thin pink line pushing above the horizon beamed into a bright yellow crescent. As the sun rose, Al nudged John awake and the two men started hiking into the hills. The liquid-filled gourd from the still was strapped to John's side.

As he chewed on cured beef, Akaka said, "This guy Hawae has been around a long time. Maybe alive when Kamehameha was king."

"Are you saying he practiced witchcraft seventy-five years ago?"

"Nobody really knows how long he's been a kahuna, or how old he is. When I was born, a few years before the massacre of the chiefs of Kauai, Hawae was already living and doing his black magic at the temple in Wailua."

John thought about this for a moment and then asked, "So why did he leave the temple?"

Akaka stopped hiking. "Don't you know your history? When the missionaries got to Hawaii, they kept working on the king, pressuring him to get rid of pagan beliefs. They got Kamehameha III to pass a law making it a crime to practice witchcraft. Once the sheriff put some of those practitioners in prison, it ended a lot of the black magic stuff. The law forced the kahuna, like Hawae, to flee to the north shore and go into hiding."

A rushing stream flumed over a rock ledge and fell in white foam into a green pool. Some of the water sprayed high into the air, misting the valley. John picked up a small stone and winged it into the sky. It tumbled through the vapors, ricocheted off a rock, and fell into the water. "Like that stone, the kahuna may have sunk below the surface, but the ripples created by old superstitions still haunt our people."

When Akaka said nothing, John continued. "You do know that Kalakaua consults a kahuna. And many others, like Haku Alapai and my wife, believe in the witch doctor's power. Maybe you believe as well?"

Akaka picked up a stick and pointed to a rainbow forming in the mist of the waterfall. He swept the wand over verdant forests, the wind moaning through rustling leaves. He waved it toward dark blue mountain crests shrouded in the grey milk of water-filled clouds. He pointed to birds soaring along crevices scoring the face of cliff walls. Akaka continued his wand's sweep over a sea covered with small caps of white. From a distance, the boom of the surf resonated into the valley, mixing with the rest of nature's sounds.

"Do you see all of this? Do you hear what I hear? This is the reason ancient Hawaiians created gods, ghosts, and kahuna. This is the reason Hawaiians still believe in black magic. John, this wild, tropical world of ours is frightening!"

John nodded. "When it's dark and the wind is howling, a superstitious person can believe in black magic. I once did. Have you ever seen Hawae do his tricks?"

Akaka breathed heavily as he trudged up the hillside trail bordering the stream. He shifted his eyes from side to side, and then, speaking in a whisper, said, "No, but I've heard the stories. How he could change himself into an animal and come to your house in the shape of a pig. How he stole hair or toenails or something personal and then looked the poor bastard in the eye, locked his brain on to him, and let the man know that he was praying him to death. In no time at all the victim would start feeling cold in his feet, then his stomach, then in his head and then, poof, he was gone."

John grabbed Akaka's arm. "You sound afraid of Hawae. Why are you guiding me to him?"

"I love Anuhai Alapai. She's family to me. And I believe you when you tell me that he poisoned her beer. Together, we'll stop this man from doing more evil to her."

For a time, the two men walked in silence, and finally came to a small clearing near the base of one of the mountains forming a side of Waialeale.

At the edge of the clearing there was a shack, a whiff of smoke escaping from its door.

"That is the house of Hawae," Akaka said, picking his way along the muddy ground. Grey vapors poured from the door, the smell pungent, nauseating.

John stepped inside and saw that the smoke was rising from leaves strewn over a low fire. In the gloom, he spied an altar with an idol upon it. Small gourds were placed around it. Kneeling at the altar was a thin man mumbling incoherent words.

"Aloha, Hawae," Akaka called from the threshold.

No answer. The kahuna continued his incantations, the pitch of his voice rising until it became a shrill and alarming song. And then he screamed, "Oh Kane, strike these enemies with your lightning. Oh Ku, send your war birds to eat out their eyes."

John took three strides closer. "Hawae, you don't frighten us. We've come to stop your poisoning of Anuhai Alapai. End your terror or I'll drag you to the sheriff and have you imprisoned."

Chanting ceased. Hawae rose. He turned to face the two men. He stared at them with a face ruddy from liquor. His sunken eyes, filled with hatred, fixed upon them. His thin lips moved, "Get out or you will be sacrifices to the gods."

"Not before you drink this beer that came from the Alapai still," John said, thrusting a gourd at the ugly man.

Hawae stuck out a bony hand, shouting as he stepped behind the altar, "I will not drink. I curse you." Reaching into a pouch, the kahuna pulled out leaves and threw them into the fire, raising a heavy smoke.

Choking from the terrible fumes, John and Akaka stumbled from the shack. When the air cleared, they went inside. Hawae was gone. They rushed out, but saw no one in the clearing. "Stay away from Wainini Beach," John yelled into the wind. "Give no more trouble to Anuhai Alapai."

His voice reverberated across the walls of the mountain: '*trouble to Anuhai Alapai, trouble to Anuhai Alapai*' echoed back.

John re-entered the shack and scattered the burnt leaves, while at the same time searching for personal items. Gathering all he could find, he put them into a bag and secured it to his waist.

Akaka watched, hands fidgeting and eyes darting about. "If you're finished, let's get out of here."

Chapter 33

Malignant spirits did not attack John and Akaka on their trek back to Anini Beach. At the Alapai compound Mahealani raced onto the roadway, tears flooding her eyes. "You're safe. I feared the kahuna would destroy you."

John took her hands placing them on his heart. "It was never a problem. How is Mama?"

"Amazing, since she stopped beer drinking she is better. The coldness is gone."

"The ape juice mixed with brew caused her illness, not the kahuna. He preyed on her mind with her hair wrapped in leaves."

Mahealani cast her eyes down. Her feet fidgeted on the grass beside the roadway. "Maybe you are right…ah, ah, I don't know."

With a sigh, John took her into his arms. "I will always protect you and the children. Gather them and we will head back to Hanalei."

"I will walk with you part of the way," Akaka said. "You are out of a job at Princeville. Cabral the Portuguese fisherman wants to start a dairy farm like he had in the old country. There are wild cows in the hills. Maybe corral some and start a business?"

"I don't know anything about that."

"Cabral does, all he needs is some land and money to get started."

"Land, I don't have. I've saved from my work, but without the Princeville job I might need to hang onto it."

"Think on it. It may be a golden opportunity."

When the family reached Sui Young's compound the Chinese rushed out to greet them. "So good you return."

"Trouble?" John asked.

"No, no, since big rain our hui think to find new place to plant rice."

Worry lines edged John's face. "You're leaving Hanalei!"

"We not, but opportunity in Anahola. Land cheap. We lease in lowland, plant rice. Lots of extra property. You build house, farm?"

John thought for a moment. "How much land? Price?"

"Maybe five hundred acres of upland. We can get cheap. Half-dollah acre."

"A month?"

"A year."

John's brow wrinkled as he thought of the prospect. *Malia's words rang in his ears: 'What Hawaiian man got? He got nothing.' Would this be an opportunity for me? I had saved some, but no more than a hundred dollars. My Hawaiian values did not permit me to beg for money.* He began to shake his head.

"You good friend, never ask for anything. Our hui help you. We no need all the land owner wants to lease. We get it. You pay back through rice profits."

John stopped the movement of his head. He glanced at his wife and saw the worry lines on her face. What Sui proposed would be risky, but would an opportunity like this ever come again? "Let me think on it."

Sui nodded. "Give me answer two days."

The family continued walking home. A late afternoon wind whipped up dust on the roadway. Nani held her mother's hand. JJ skipped ahead, happily slapping the tall grass growing by the river. "You want the land. How can we do it? We only have enough to pay for the family. You give up rice profits, we have nothing? Farming hard work, long time before grow anything to eat or sell."

John chewed on a stalk of olena, its yellow juice coating his tongue. "This is good medicine for all kinds of ailments. Its sharp taste also makes me think. Today we have nothing more than what we make with our hands. But if we could grow something, like I did in the past, and sell it, we could make money."

"That's not the way of our people."

"I'm thinking we need to change."

"But taro is sacred. It's something you do not sell, but share with others."

John paused in his walk and fixed his eyes on his wife. "I'm not talking about growing taro. No. It's raising cows for milk and meat. There is nothing sacred about those animals. Nothing that Hawaiians shared with others in the past."

"Cows! What do you know about cows?"

"Nothing, except they're big, but Cabral knows something. I'm going to talk to him."

Mahealani sighed. "If you do this, let me know how you plan to feed us?"

"The only way the haole makes money is taking risks. I saw that in whaling. I saw that in sugar cane growing. Yes, you fail like Princeville Plantation and Kalakaua's mill in Kapaa. But if you can make it, then—"

"You are a dreamer," Mahealani interrupted. She sighed, then said, "If things get too difficult for us we can always go back to Anini. Plenty fish and taro."

"And the kahunas are all gone," John smiled.

"Don't torment me with your Christianity."

"I do not mean to. But Hawaii has changed from ancient times. We must change with it. Something has been nagging me for a long time, ever since I learned about capitalism. You must spend money to make money. If we don't take chances, we will always have our feet in the mud."

"You want to climb out of the taro patch and act like the rich, not caring for anybody or sharing with others what you have."

"Don't pass judgment on me too quickly. Let's get ahead in the world. I won't forget our values."

Chapter 34

In the days that followed, John, Cabral, and Akaka surveyed the land that Sui Young proposed to lease. The Portuguese deemed it prime land for cattle raising and dairy farming. A deal was made with the Chinese. John invested a hundred dollars he had saved, and the Hawaiians went to work to fence the property, build corrals, structures, and acquire cattle.

John received a summons to meet with Gordon, the manager of Kilauea Plantation. In his best clothes, clean-shaven, and haircut, John came to the mill office. Unlike a previous occasion, the clerk showed him some deference and ushered him into the manager's room.

Gordon rose from his desk and extended his hand. The men shook. "Cigar?" Gordon asked, offering John an open humidor stacked with tightly-wrapped tobacco cylinders.

"Thank you for your offer. I don't smoke, but appreciate your generosity."

There was a pause in conversation before Gordon spoke again. "This plantation is stocked with Chinese and a few Hawaiian workers. I recall your mention of Fijians, and Portuguese coming to work for us. I'm amazed that you knew this, but that is not important. My partners and I realize with all these new people who may be coming to work, there could be serious friction between them. After much discussion, we have decided to hire you."

"You'll place me in charge of your security? What do you intend to pay?"

Surprised by the sudden demand, Gordon blustered, "I would think you would be happy to have a new job. You've been out of work for months. You must be hurting for money."

They need me, John thought. He decided to act as if he didn't want the work. Watching the Chinese, he had learned about bargaining. He would be pake. "Much has happened since I saw you last. Working on a new enterprise in Anahola, hundreds of acres of land involved."

"Oh, you have another source of income besides the rice fields. If you don't want the work—".

"I have the finest credentials for security work of anyone on the island. You've seen Low's recommendation. I know that I'm the best that you can find. The government will not solve your labor problems." *There, I did it. I went from 'dumb Hawaiian', abandoned humility, and advertised what I could do.*

Gordon reached into his cigar case, removed one of the stogies, lit it, inhaled, and blew smoke into the room. "You're a much different chap than the fellow I met months ago, but are you just bluster, without any fire in you, like so many Hawaiians? With all these races coming here you will need to be tough enough to keep men under control."

This is the big test, John thought: *Would I be easy-going and let incidents pass or take the steps needed to stop trouble before it started*? "In Hanalei I ended a war before it started. I did what had to be done to stop a fire from destroying a mill. I saved a king from assassination by acting quickly. When it comes to physical confrontations I am not afraid to face anyone and deal with the trouble. You need what I can give."

Gordon puffed several times on his cigar, smoke filling the room as the tip glowed. He stroked his chin, then said, "You are different from the others of your race that I have met. Being confident and outspoken in your abilities is quite unusual. What did they pay you at Princeville?"

"Thirty dollars a month."

"Too much, we will pay twenty-five."

"Make it sixty, I need help to do the job."

"Outrageous. Managers get a hundred a month. Thirty-five."

"My information is that they get more than that. Besides I'm worth it. Fifty-five."

"Forty and not a penny more."

"Make it forty-five and we have a deal."

Gordon puffed on his cigar. Squinted through the smoke. "Forty!"

"Forty-five and not a penny less."

Pursing his lips, staring at John, the manager said, "Done, at forty-five dollars a month. You drive a hard bargain."

"I know that you need me."

John left the office, and as soon he was out of sight, raced to Anini Beach. He found his wife, lifted her in the air, and said, "No more worries. We are in at Kilauea Plantation."

Chapter 35

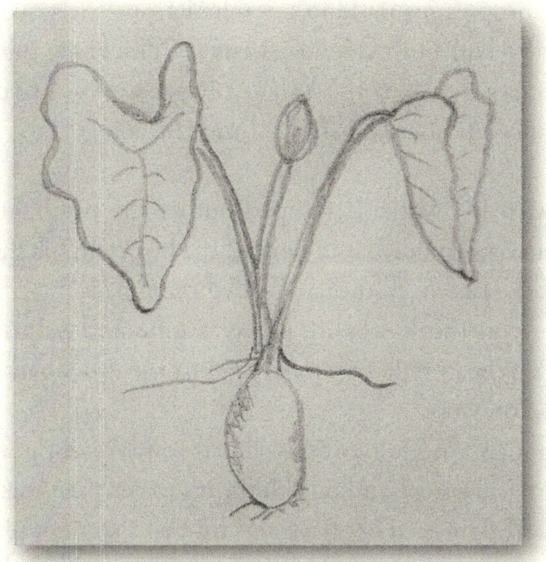

Taro Plant

Kilauea, 1883

Water from the river sluiced down a ditch into an acre of mud. With a taro plant in his hand, John said, "JJ, break the offshoot from the corm and stick it into the wet dirt. If we work hard, we'll be done before nightfall and we can go fishing."

JJ's eyes sparkled with the possibilities and the eight-year-old began tearing off shoots and thrusting them haphazardly into the mud.

"Take your time. Make sure the green crown of the plant is well into the water before you plant the next one."

John lifted his eyes from the taro field, surveying seven acres of land he had purchased with his profits from the rice fields, his earnings from his security job at Kilauea Plantation, and the money coming in from the dairy farm. The acreage had been bought from an old Hawaiian chief, and attorney Joshua Kanakoa had made sure that John had secured a proper patent for the property. His land stretched from the government road to the sea. On it he had built a home, pens for chickens, pigs, and cattle. A long irrigation canal dug to the Kilauea River watered two acres of yams, sweet potatoes, calabashes, vegetables, and the acre of taro that he had just planted.

Finished with his work, JJ jumped out of the patch, releasing a laugh when his father reached down and hoisted the boy onto his shoulders. As they headed toward the beach, Mahealani called them back.

"Where do you think you are going? Come and help me." She turned back to the task of beating her pounder against the inner bark of the mulberry bush that rested on wood.

"You are not smart." John observed, his son wriggling on his shoulders. "Go to the plantation store and buy cloth. It's easier than mashing bark!"

Mahealani straightened her back and rubbed a sore spot low on her spine. "Since you got that security job with Kilauea Plantation and the rice money, all you think about is spending it. Spit on your hands and come pound the bark." When he laughed, she added, "*Kapa* is the best cloth. When I design, and dye it, you'll see how beautiful it is."

Mahealani's joy at having a new home made John happy. He glanced around the solid structure made of wood and raised on stilts to protect it from floods, fleas, centipedes, and scorpions that plagued so many grass shacks. He looked back at his wife, knowing very well that even if there was no job to do, Mahealani would invent one.

"Moana wants our help at the beach. After we're finished, JJ and I will go fishing."

Grumbling, Mahealani pointed her beater at John. "All right, you go. But don't you sit around drinking beer and telling stories. Keep an eye on your father, JJ. I want a full report of what went on at the beach."

JJ twisted his mouth. "Mom, don't make me into a snitch."

Mahealani knew that the boy would not lie. On the other hand, telling the truth would not make him one of the men. "Fine," she grumbled. "Have a good time while I stay here and work." Before she could change her mind, John pulled JJ from his shoulders and they rushed downhill heading for the fishing shack by the sea.

After helping Moana with some repairs, John retrieved fishing equipment. Mahealani had abandoned her work of pounding kapa and had come to the beach to investigate what the men were doing. When she saw the two spears John had in his hand, she complained, "Don't take the boy beyond the reef."

John kissed her forehead, and tenderly stroked her long hair. "I'm going to get the nenue you wanted. We can sprinkle it with limu and eat it raw, just how you like it."

Mahealani smiled. "Good, get me some fat ones, the kind with the yellow belly. But watch the boy," she added, a warning creeping into her voice. "Don't let him go deep. Keep him close to shore."

JJ sighed. "Oh, Ma, don't worry, I can take care of myself." He held up a spear. "Look what Dad made for me." He pointed to the barb near its sharp tip. "It swivels up and down, so the fish are hooked as soon as I spear them."

Mahealani gave John a glaring look and said to her son, "Don't poke yourself. Once that's in you it won't come out."

Beyond the line of waves breaking onto the fringing reef, the depth of water increased as the island shelved downward into deep-sea trenches. John directed JJ toward a large crevice in the reef. Fish swam in, out, around, and through it. "Nenue," John said. "No unnecessary motions. Movement frightens them. Tread the water. They are curious and come to see who may threaten their home. When they turn, submerge, and shoot."

A dozen fish darted toward them, their lidless eyes staring, caudal fins thrusting them through the water. Within six feet, the horde turned their broad silver-scaled bodies. John's spear shot out, skewering a four-pound fish that jiggled and whirled as it fought to escape the harpoon. In his excitement, JJ missed.

John strung the nenue through the gills with an iron needle attached to a long slender cord. He pushed the fish fifteen feet along the cord to a wooden float bobbing on the surface. As they tread water John said, "Don't worry. They will come back. Breathe, duck your head, and watch." The fish returned and John skewered another. His son thrust, but failed, only nicking his target. Finally, after John had caught six, JJ speared his first. The boy screamed, "Look, Dad." He held his catch above the water, the fish flopping against his clenched fist.

"Good job." He was happy for his son's joy. Earlier in the day, JJ had learned to be a planter, a back-breaking, dirty, job that the boy disliked. Now he had become a fisherman, a cleaner, more exciting activity. But John knew it had greater dangers than working in the mud.

He pointed to a large underwater reef thrusting through a carpet of white sand. There were fingers of pink stone growing from it and several mounds of yellow brain coral. Tiny fish, striped in multi-colored hues of green, red, and blue flitted about the craggy rocks. Particles of the brown moss they fed on floated lazily toward the surface. In and out of slits within the reef swam schools of red fish, their round gelatin eyes swiveling from side to side. Tiny whiskers, like thin fingers, drooped from their jaws, flicking the sand, searching for food.

"Kumu," John said. "When it sees you, it could continue to feed or swim into a cut in the reef. If it does, wait. It will come out again."

They dove toward the isolated reef and the red goat fish. John watched JJ easily spear a kumu and kick toward the surface, bubbles escaping from his smiling lips. He burst through the surface and crowed, "Look, Dad. I hit it on my first thrust."

John smiled, stringing the catch. JJ dove again and for the next few minutes he kept surfacing with a fish struggling on his spear. "This is great," he yelled each time he came to the top. His excitement made John happy, but it was tempered by his worry as he watched the greenish offal from the speared fish swirl in the sea current and flow into the deeper blue water.

JJ surfaced some distance away, a large red goat fish fixed on his spear. It spanked the sea with its caudal fin. From the wound in the middle of its body, a thin red stream of blood flowed. "JJ," John called. The boy swam to his father.

"Hurry up, Dad," JJ screamed. "String the fish." The boy fumbled with the flopping animal, his fingers slipping from its gills as he tried to widen the mouth of the fish to insert the iron needle.

"JJ, we must go."

"Why? I'm having fun."

"Take a breath and look under the water." John pointed to a long grey tube slithering along the bottom. "That's Mano. The shark smells blood in the water. It makes him hungry. Don't panic. Just keep your eye on him as we move to the shoreline reef."

Mano – shark

John saw his son trembling as the predator angled along the coral, a large black pupil surrounded by an orb of white, staring malevolently at the boy. Its jaws gaped, drawing in water that flushed out through gills behind its mouth. Dozens of sharp, pointed teeth ringed its long grey snout. John passed the speared fish to his son. "Hold tight. Don't let Mano eat them. Swim toward the surf line."

"Where you going, Dad?" JJ screamed, but John had no time to explain as he disappeared underwater.

The shark angled along the sea bottom, swimming to come between JJ and shallower water. John grabbed nubs of rock thrusting above the sand, pulling himself along the bottom. In the other hand, he gripped his spear, pointing it at the shark. A school of remora fish flitting above their host clamped down on the snout of the predator. The monstrous animal thrust its tail sideways and sped into the deep blue of the ocean.

John glided along the rising sea bottom, surfacing just at the foaming line of breakers. "Swim to me," he yelled. He saw JJ release his spear and watched it whirl to the sand floor twenty feet below him. Flailing his arms and legs, the boy struggled to reach safety. The fish cord trailed behind him and twisted around a leg, forcing JJ into a modified kick. Despite his son's troubles, John saw that the boy would not release the fish line to the ocean. JJ's pride in securing their catch was equal to that of his father.

Problems mounted. The weight and pull of the fish acted like a sea anchor. John saw his son's distress and swam toward his son. As he got closer, he saw JJ's hand striking coral. As JJ grasped the rock, a great black fin sliced through the water, dipped, and the long predator's body turned just beyond JJ's flailing feet. John flung himself at the shark.

With a sudden jerk, the needle and cord yanked from JJ's teeth, almost toppling him backward. A half-dozen speared fish rose with an incoming wave, flapping aimlessly in the water. The shark's fin headed toward the deep, blood and torn flesh trailing behind it. John yelled, "JJ, you okay?"

Gulping air, the shaking boy nodded his head.

"Get on the reef." John seized the broken line, tied it, and threaded floating fish onto the cord. A flock of shearwater birds skimmed the sea, their bodies dipping from side to side as they soared just above the surface. With strong beats of their wings, they rose rapidly toward the clouds. JJ screamed, "Mano." He pointed to where the birds were rising into the sky. A dark fin knifed through the water heading toward them.

"Wedge yourself among the rocks," John yelled, pulling the line of fish into him. He swam to JJ and together they crammed themselves into a jagged crevice in the reef, its edges barely poking above the water. The predator sliced by their shelter, its fins furrowing the sea sending low waves rippling into them.

Hunkered down between the rocks, John and JJ watched the shark swim around their shelter and slide into a shallow channel leading to shore. Whipping its body, the great fish found a wide opening in the coral reef, swam around the beleaguered pair, then darted out to sea. "If I let him have our fish, he might go away," John said.

JJ shivered. He looked at his father and shook his head. John smiled. He was proud of his son, a true fisherman. He also knew that if he fed the big fish it might go into a feeding frenzy and attack them despite the protection of their reef shelter.

The shark returned. It began a series of taunting passes, swimming close, circling, returning to the deep, and then charging back. When its massive body moved in the shallows, it created a wake of low waves that rolled over John and his son. With each return, the shark tried to move closer to them. John clasped a shivering JJ to his chest, the fish they had caught floating beside them. His spear was poised to strike if the predator thrust its snout into their shelter.

After what seemed like endless menacing passes, the predator fanned its large tail and disappeared. John held JJ, waiting until he was certain that the shark would not return. When he judged the moment to be safe, he pointed and said, "Swim into that narrow channel. Head for the beach, I'll be behind you, watching."

Father and son reached the shore where they sat on the sand for a long moment. Neither spoke. John stood. JJ rose, wrapped his arm around his dad, and they trudged home.

John knew better than to expect JJ to say nothing. The moment they arrived at the seashore shack, the boy graphically described his near-death experience to his mother.

"You're lucky your son still has his legs," Mahealani said, her voice threatening, yet tinged with fear. "How could you let the boy get into such danger?"

As he pounded poi nearby, Moana broke through the tension between the parents. "Eh, sister, that kind of stuff happens. It's all part of becoming a man. I'll clean the fish and cut up the nenue. Make it raw just as you like it." Mahealani stopped grumbling and returned to her work.

Chapter 36

Water meandered over rocks and cataracts, some sluicing into a new irrigation ditch that fed the plants and animals owned by the Tana family. John banked rocks against the sides of the sluice, strengthening the artificial channel that diverted river water to his farm. Beside him, JJ placed more rocks to aid the flow of water.

As he wiped moisture from his face, John studied his son for some moments. "Haku Alapai tells me that you flub your knotting when you're making net. He says you're always daydreaming, never paying attention to what he teaches you. What's wrong?"

JJ shifted his feet, avoiding his father's eyes. "I don't know, Dad. Ever since the shark almost got me, I can't think of fishing without seeing that great big wild thing swimming circles around us. I'm scared to put my head under the water because Mano and his big teeth might be hiding in the shadows."

The boy had a crease running across his forehead and he seemed close to tears. "I can't think of making net, when all I want is the biggest spear in the world to fight Mano. One day, I won't be afraid and then we will battle." His fears revealed, the boy stood, thrusting his fist toward the sea.

John lifted his son until their foreheads met and their eyes locked. "Someday, you will overcome Mano and then your worry of what might come from the darkness of the deep will disappear forever." John set him down, they turned and headed for home.

John found Mahealani working on furniture coverings in the living room. He padded up to her and swept his wife into his arms, dancing her around the room. "We are going to make lots of money."

Mahealani tried to regain her footing. "John, stop!" she insisted, catching her breath, her large belly protruding with child. "I'm not light on my feet like you are. Maybe since you're so successful you'll carry this baby for us."

"I would if I could," John smiled, and raised the hem of Mahealani's blouse and caressed her belly. He kissed it and said, "I just wanted to let you know, I love you very much."

"All right, now that I know you love me and the baby, what do you mean, 'we are going to make lots of money'?"

"Cabral's dairy is very successful and Ito is going to start a pig farm there. Our Anahola land is getting more valuable every day and we have nothing to do but get rich."

"What are we going to do with more money? We have enough to live on."

"We can get more land. I have dreamed of starting a co-operative farm where poor Hawaiians and Chinese can come to find a new life."

Mahealani settled herself to the floor, returning to her work. "Be sure you tend to your family first. If you keep playing with me, it will get bigger." She rubbed her tummy and then smiled. "Of course, you can always sleep in the spare room and dream of your co-operative farm. That will stop children from coming."

The next day, Mahealani and JJ headed outside to begin their morning chores. When they arrived at the animal enclosures next to the growing fields, they found devastation: shattered pens, taro plants trashed. "Get your father!" Mahealani screamed, gripping a fence post for support.

John heard her yell. Pulling on his shirt, he ran to the west side of his property. Mahealani held onto a post, staring at a destroyed field and a half-dozen fat porkers wallowing in the mud chewing on uprooted plants.

"What could have done all this?" she asked with a groan.

John surveyed the damage, JJ by his side. "A wild animal, I think. The plantation manager told me yesterday that they were having cane fields trashed in the night by something big. No one has seen it, but I'm guessing rogue cattle or a huge boar." He inspected some of the damage. "Judging by this debris, I'd say it was a boar."

Mahealani frowned, her hand pressed against her cheek as she leaned into her husband. "Why would a wild pig come from the mountains to trample our farm? It doesn't make sense for an animal to come through the forests, over the hills, and across the cane fields, just to attack us."

"Maybe the boar was looking for a sweetheart?" he suggested playfully, giving his wife a little embrace. "Let me count the pigs," he added.

Mahealani was not amused. Concern clouded her face. "Maybe we've offended someone? What if it's a ghost, sent by a kahuna? Lono is god of the pigs. We should make sacrifices. Beg him to end this attack." Mahealani wept as JJ patted her arm.

"Nonsense. This damage was done by something real, not a ghost." John sighed. "Stop this crazy talk."

Mahealani sobbed. "You don't believe. But think of your family. What will happen if the death-dealer attacks the baby? No, we must pray to the gods." Her weeping frightened JJ. He looked at his father, uncertainty in his face.

"The worship of the old gods is over. Put aside your fears. JJ, ask Moana and Haku Alapai to come and help clean up. I'm going to talk to Al and see if I can borrow one of his dogs."

Two nights passed and Kaulana, a watchdog John got from Akaka, did not howl. On the third evening following the attack, Mahealani polished a bottle gourd in the family living room. With a sigh, she said, "I spoke to Mama. She told me she had strange sensations during the night. A frigid wind swept through the house and turned her feet cold. Her stomach churned. I remember being sick." She put down the gourd and said, "I'm afraid."

John massaged her shoulders. Speaking softly, he said, "I'm here to protect you. Remember that superstition creates fear. Believe in Christ and you will overcome your fright."

"I know that you will do what you can to protect us, but I had a terrible dream last night. Fiery eyes bore into my body and ugly hands reached out to grasp our baby. I forced myself awake, sweating, and afraid."

John kissed Mahealani. "An uhane is not real. Imagination creates it." John felt Mahealani's body relax under his touch. "It was a stray pig without enough to eat in the mountains that trashed our farm."

After they went to bed, a bright ring of clouds pulsed around a glowing moon. As it dropped below the mountains, Kaulana erupted with vicious barking.

John jumped into his trousers and ran outside, a Winchester rifle and a flaming kerosene torch in his hands. The light flickered in the early morning breeze, stabs of flame melding into weird shadows dancing like ghosts over the ground.

Sounds of grunting, growling, and thrashing beat into the night, drawing John to the edge of the farm. A mournful yowl spiked the darkness, mixing with the heavy snorting of a pig. John raced to the sounds. They ended, replaced by an eerie clatter.

The flame of John's torch illuminated the watchdog, his lungs rattling in the throes of death. Above the animal stood a huge black boar, its sharp tusks and snout smeared with blood. John stopped, holding his breath. For moments, man and animal glared at each other, John's blood running cold as a pair of malevolent eyes stared at him. The boar pawed the ground, preparing to charge. John raised his Winchester. Behind him Moana yelled, "Oh, my God!" In an instant, the beast turned, fleeing into the darkness.

The next day, a shaken John Tana received permission from the plantation manager to take time off to hunt the pig. With the help of Cabral, he contacted a Russian, Abraham Karlov, who had the dogs and expertise to lead the hunt.

"Just call me Brudda." Karlov laughed when the two men met. "My baby sister could never say *brother*, just *brudda*, so that's why the nickname. I should tell you, I don't use guns, just knives and my dogs."

Chapter 37

Ancient Heiau Stones

Four days after the boar's attack, John and Karlov followed a trail leading into the mountains. A pack of six hunting dogs crisscrossed in front of them, sniffing the wind, seeking the scent of a feral pig. The men followed the pack as it crossed the Kilauea and Kalihiwai streams, and headed toward the base of the mountains.

Their machetes slashed through thick shrubs until they reached a grass plateau that backed into the mountainside. In it stood a grass shack. As the dogs ran about the structure, John said, "Damn, this is where Hawae lives."

Karlov shot John a startled look. "You know the guy who lives here?"

"He's a kahuna. I had a run-in with him in the past."

"Kahuna! One of those death-dealing devil worshipers?"

John nodded. "I hope you don't believe in that black magic stuff?"

Karlov shook his head. "Nah, only ignorant people buy into witches and dark arts. It gives those dummies a feeling of power. I spit on this kahuna crap." The man emphasized this by sending a stream of tobacco juice into the grass house.

John bridled at his words. "My wife's not ignorant, yet she believes in the kahuna. She tried to discourage me from going on this adventure saying, 'Pig is soul of Hawae. Leave him alone. Pray to the gods'."

"So why did you hire me to get this creature?"

"It is to prove to her that the damn thing is mortal like you and me. Yet, now that your dogs have brought us here, I don't know…" John's voice trailed off.

Karlov shrugged. "There is no sense in having cold feet. Let's find out if this guy's at home."

The shack was empty, yet someone had occupied it. Sparkling coals from a nearly dead fire gave slim light to the interior. When Karlov emerged from the shack he ordered, "Search for spoor."

The hounds ran about the clearing, hunting the damp ground, shrubs, and trees, checking for signs of a pig. Finally, two dogs milled around a tree, barking.

"Come here," Karlov said, inspecting the tree trunk. "See the scraping on the bark? And that black bristle? A big pig has rubbed his body on this tree." Beneath it were large three-toed hoof prints that led into thick woods and bushes. "Get out your machete, we've got chopping to do."

Karlov moved into the thickets adding, "The dogs will try to work their way through the bush and lead us to whatever left those prints."

John chopped at the thick bushes, sweating with the effort. "What happens when we find the boar?"

"The closest man to him sticks a knife between his front legs and into his lung or heart."

"Wait, you're the expert, why don't you kill the creature?"

Karlov stopped and turned around. "Look, Tana, we have one chance at this animal. The dogs may not be able to hold it until I come up. Remember this: when it attacks, the pig can only see the dogs. This'll give one of us a few seconds to step into its side, cut his throat or stick a knife between his leg and chest. Any other strike will hurt it, not kill it. And don't forget that it's covered with wirehair, which is as tough as iron."

"And if I can't cut its throat or stick the knife in the right place, what then?"

Karlov smiled. "Then pray, my brother, that the animal doesn't split you in two." The Russian laughed and patted John's back. "If you can't slit the throat or get to the heart, try to cut its back legs. It'll make the pig fall, and then you can get him. Just remember, the hog is stupid, he always runs straight. So, if you attack him from the side, he won't get you."

John wondered, *how stupid can this pig be if it was smart enough to recognize a rifle and run away from it?*

As they chopped through thick, heavy shrubs, their long-sleeved shirts and pants torn by thorns and twigs, the men came to a brook. The dogs ran along its bank, growling, then moved upstream. "This way," Karlov pointed, following close behind. Soon he paused and sniffed. "The air isn't moving," he said. "It stinks of rotted wood and dead leaves." Mosquitoes rose from a fetid carpet of decaying mush, buzzing about, searching for patches of uncovered skin and fresh blood.

John slapped at the dark cloud circling his head. "Move on!" he yelled, dodging to avoid the bugs. Somewhere ahead, a dog barked and there was the sound of breaking wood.

"Let's go!"

The men slid and slithered, and forced their way through the underbrush and into a peaceful glade. From a source above, shrouded in clouds, a long rope of water fell into a mountainside pool. Spouts thrust up by the plunging water splashed onto the rocks that ringed the pond. Over the ages, the waterfall had carved a long wedge into the mountain. At the base of the wedge lay the opening of a grotto, its entry covered by a mass of bending ferns sprouting from wet rock. Moss covered the mountainside. From that green thickness grew sprigs of purple flowers that trailed into the pool. Scattered about were Hawaiian hibiscus, their flowering white petals open as they drank from the weak sunlight filtering through the trees above the pond.

John stared at the beautiful scene, distracted from the hunt. The dogs howled, and he heard a wild thrashing in the bush.

"My hounds are onto something. Come."

The two men pushed into the undergrowth, slamming into sticky spider webs strung between branches. They slipped into a small bog, wading through green slime toward the sound of the yelping animals.

"See the big log ahead of us, the one by the busted stump? I can hear my boys snarling beyond it. John, go to the right. I'll go left and we'll see what's on the other side."

John pushed through liquid dank with floating green muck and climbed out of the water and onto the bank. Beyond the fallen tree, he heard vicious growling mixed with staccato grunting. He stepped around the trunk, discovering a path lined on both sides by dense bushes. At the end of it, backed against a great rock, stood an enormous beast, its mouth frothing, its body covered with wiry black bristles. Cloven hoofs pawed the ground, flinging dirt and dead leaves into the air. John stared into red eyes that glared at him.

A hound charged the boar, aiming for its throat. With a jerk of its ivory tusks the animal impaled the dog, and flung the yelping animal into the bush. Other dogs fastened their teeth onto the legs and flank of the beast. The boar managed to turn its snout, bloodshot eyes piercing into John. In one violent movement, the boar shook off the dogs and charged.

John drew his knife, a weapon he knew was too pitiful to meet this attack. The trail was narrow, blocking his escape. He knew that if he turned and ran, the hog would catch and impale him.

Before the animal struck, one of the dogs fastened itself onto its back leg. Another dog shot past John and bit into the pig's throat. The creature stumbled and swerved, thrown off by the attacks. Razor-sharp hog's hair brushed John's leg, shredding his pants, cutting into his flesh, forcing him to his knees. The stench of the animal choked him, clouding his eyes with tears.

Just beyond John, the boar tried to shake off the dogs. When a third fastened onto its leg, the hog tilted, exposing its belly. Half-blinded by the stink of the beast, John plunged his knife into the crease between its shoulder and chest, thrusting his weapon deep into its lungs.

With a massive shriek, the black pig shook, flinging away two of the attacking dogs. With John's knife buried into its side, the boar rose, smashing into the brush, dragging a dog with him.

Karlov charged up. John stood in the center of a blood-splattered path. "Don't chase that guy into the bush. He's not dead yet. Right now, he's more dangerous than he'll ever be."

In moments, a bloodied dog emerged from the bushes, limping toward its master, head hung low. Karlov inspected him, finding no serious injuries.

"Look, Brudda, we've waited long enough for that thing to die. I'm going in there to get him."

"Dangerous, let the dogs do it."

"You've already lost two dogs. That's enough." John swung his machete, hacking at the brush, enlarging the opening the hog had made. He followed its bloody trail, finding passage through the shrubs easy. In some places, he could crawl with a minimum of cutting.

John pushed himself through the growth into the mountainside glade. Dark, red ripples shimmered toward him. The blood-colored water stretched the length of the pool to the grotto at the base of the mountain.

Karlov came up and pointed toward the cave. "Look at what's lying on the rocks. Isn't that your knife?"

Bewildered, John stepped into the cold red water and pushed his way toward the grotto. The weeping ferns covering the entrance suddenly brushed upward and a winged body flew through them. Sailing across the pond, a brown owl struggled to gain height.

It clawed onto a low branch and turned its bloodshot yellow eyes toward John Tana. For many seconds, pueo and man stared at each other. The owl hooted, then relaxed its hold on the limb, spread its wings, and glided into the forest.

Pueo

In the dying light of the day, Karlov joined John at the edge of the pool studying the mouth of the low cave. The Russian steadied himself on John's arm and bent low, peering inside. "I'm sure you finished him. It's probably dying in the cave. It's getting dark. Let's get out of here."

John's instincts told him to go into the grotto and finish the job, but he deferred to Karlov's wisdom. They hiked back along the trail and came to the witch doctor's shack. The sun had set minutes earlier and everything was cast in darkness. Without knowing why, John groped around in the murk of the sorcerer's hut. The coals of the fire still sparkled. On the altar above the weak light, lay a lump. He reached beyond the burning wood and grasped the object. As he closed his hand over it, a slender stick pricked his flesh.

John left the shack unwrapping a bundle of ape leaves. Inside, he found a nut-brown rag doll. Penetrating its belly was a green-coated sliver of bamboo. "Oh, my God, we must get home!"

The men stumbled through the darkness, desperate to reach the Tana compound. It was past midnight when they arrived, bruised and bone-tired. Lanterns of flaming kerosene flooded the grounds and a terrible wailing came from John's home. He barely contained his own cries as he rushed inside.

The family stood weeping. Mahealani lay on her bed. Her eyes closed, her skin pale. Blood soaked a blanket. In it lay a still-born child. She woke, saw John, and screamed, "Our baby is dead. You killed him. You did not believe in the power of kahuna. Oh, woe is our family. Only evil can come to it."

Chapter 38

Makena Mountain lay bare and black, its massive sixteen-hundred-foot bulk thrust into the ocean like a clenched fist. It stood as the first of many barriers protecting the hidden jewel of Kalalau Valley.

Fire sticks poured from its peak, flaming wood splintering against the rocks as they fell, creating embers that plunged in a waterfall of fire into the sea. As the *Kilauea* sailed past, passengers stood transfixed, others gasped, at the sight of the fiery torrent sparkling as it fell and then dying with sizzles of steam as it hit the tossing waves.

At the rail of the *Kilauea*, Princess Liliuokalani leaned closer to John and whispered, "Thank you, Mr. Tana, for arranging this exhibition of fire. It is indeed an awesome display."

John paused, thinking back on the events of the morning. He had been assigned to protect the regent on her visit to the north coast of Kauai. At the ceremonies earlier in the day, she had driven the first spike into the rails that would end the hauling of cane to the Kilauea mill by oxen. No longer would the supply of raw product be limited to the three miles that the animals could pull a full load. With railroad tracks laid for miles into the hills, the iron locomotive and its boxcars could transport ten times more than the animals over longer distances.

"Hailama puts on a wonderful show. His fireworks are spectacular, but not as awesome as what is happening in Kilauea and the new train that we saw this morning."

"It's a pretty toy, Mr. Tana."

John chuckled as he remembered the tiny, seven-foot tall and four-foot wide engine. Despite its small size, he knew that it would make the sugar people rich.

“I fear that the machine we saw this morning will change the life of our land and our people forever.”

“It’s not just this train that will change things for us. It’s all the new methods and equipment for processing raw cane into sugar. It means more land will be taken from the Hawaiian and more labor will be imported to slave in the fields. Your brother’s reciprocity treaty will not only end Hawaii as we know it, it will also push us into the arms of the United States.”

His next words were interrupted by screams coming from the beach. A rogue wind blew hot sparks toward spectators on the shore. Musicians on board the *Kilauea* began to strum their guitars, and a deep male voice sang a Hawaiian love song. From the shore, other guitars picked up the tune, a woman’s voice singing across the water, answering the man’s love call.

Hailama continued flinging his burning wood over the mountain’s edge as a girl approached the princess and placed a flower lei around her shoulders. Behind her came a young man, who slipped a necklace of burnished kukui nuts around John’s neck, falling firebrands reflected on their sleek surface.

“Thank you again, Mr. Tana, for this event. I will see you in Honolulu and after a time we will be off to Molokai.”

Later that night, John returned home. Mahealani sat huddled in a chair on the veranda, her long hair spread over her body, her face haggard. John bent down, kissing her forehead. “I need to talk to you.”

His wife looked at him, sighed, and then returned to watching the sea. Folding her hands, she said, “What is it?”

John gazed at her, slender, still beautiful, yet aging too quickly. The attack of the feral pig and the premature death of her son haunted her. She blamed herself for failing to make proper offerings to Lono, god of pigs. She blamed John for believing in the Christian God, and not the gods of their ancestors.

“I must leave for Honolulu and then Molokai. I’ll be gone for a few weeks.”

Mahealani looked without answering, her expression unchanging and detached.

John took her folded hands in his. “Princess Liliuokalani has been touring the islands and wants me to provide her with security for a gala party in

Honolulu, and later when she visits the leper colony on Molokai." He did not add that many Hawaiians were unhappy over the imprisonment of lepers in Kalawao. It had been the subject of many angry discussions.

Mahealani dropped her eyes as she pulled her hands from John's. "It's sad to take people from their families and cast them into that awful place. It is death. I know the pain that comes from death."

"Set aside your dark thoughts." John stroked her hair, and then cupping her face in his hands, mixing his breath with hers. "You have many people who love you. Come away from your pain and see the happiness that is around you."

Mahealani smiled, her eyes lighting for a moment with a sparkle. "You are a special man, John Tana. No other husband would put up with my sadness. Go and do your duty to our princess. When you return, I will be better." Then she stood, holding onto John, who pulled her head onto his chest and caressed her. "I would like to spend the night with Anuhai."

John nodded. The next day, he left for Honolulu.

Chapter 39

Honolulu

At mid-morning, the day after he arrived in the capitol of Hawaii, John left Ah Sam's restaurant heading for the Hawaiian Hotel. He knew he could walk the streets of Honolulu without fear. Joshua, his attorney, had assured him that a warrant for his arrest no longer existed. Maria had absolved him of any wrongdoing, and the escapade with Shaw had not resulted in any charges against him. He asked about Maria's welfare and learned the young girl had left for France with her father. He knew nothing more.

At the Hawaiian Hotel, John asked for the dining room and its chief cook and was directed to a six-foot-four-inch giant. Standing next to Joseph Still, the head chef, John asked, "Other than this pantry door and the back door to the alley, what are the entryways into your kitchen?"

"There are none," Still answered.

"Besides yourself, who else is permitted into this area?"

"I have six serving men, two busboys, and a sous chef."

"Can you vouch for each of them?"

Still took little time to reply, "Yes, I can. Mr. Tana, could you tell me what you're worried about? I realize that you're very thorough, but nothing has ever happened while I've been the chef at this hotel."

John felt frustrated that this man refused to understand the dangers to the princess. "Mr. Still, it is my job to be thorough. Princess Liliuokalani will soon leave for Molokai and the leper colony, and many Hawaiians are angry that family members are shipped there. Some seek to assassinate the heir to our throne. Let's just say that I don't want anything to happen while I'm on duty." When he saw how Still listened, absorbed in his concerns, he wondered if this man could become a friend.

While making his security checks, John's heart skipped as Leinani entered the dining room. The eyes of every man followed her as she passed through. When she saw John, a smile lit her face. She moved to him, a tall gentleman following close behind. Without hesitation, she kissed him on the cheek and said to her companion. "James, this is John Tana. He is the one I told you of, who rescued me from an awful sea captain, and saved me from a crude man." She finished the introduction: "This is my husband, James Kingsley."

For a moment, the two appraised each other. Kingsley's eyes came even with his, but John thought his features delicate, his face soft, and his hands un-calloused. They were pale, aristocratic, and had never known hard work.

After a long moment, Kingsley said, "Delighted to meet you. Are you a guest at this party?"

John returned the smile. "Just a hired policeman. I've been providing security for the princess and I'll soon accompany her to Molokai."

Kingsley nodded, as if interested in what John said. "I certainly hope she doesn't need protection. But I'm certain she's safe in your hands."

Leinani turned to her husband, her face animated with expectation. "James, I would love to have John visit with us. We could catch up on the many years since we've been apart. Could we invite him to dinner sometime soon?"

Before Kingsley could answer, a couple joined them.

"Oh, my Hawaiian Lothario!" gushed June Tucker, placing a hand on John's shoulder and kissing him on the lips. "Thank you for saving my life."

With a start, John recognized the two people he had rescued. He stole a glance at Leinani whose face flushed crimson.

"You know each other?" Kingsley asked.

"Oh yes, we do. We met in the moonlight on the beach at Kalihiwai, where Mr. Tana shared his knowledge of Shakespeare and Don Quixote. I was amazed at this Hawaiian man's education. He must have had a great teacher."

John smiled at Leinani, giving her a slight bow. "I have my former cousin to thank for all that I know of poetry, literature, and famous lovers."

Leinani frowned, her posture stiffened. For a moment, there was an awkward silence. Allen Tucker said, "Besides all his accomplishments, Mr. Tana is a hero. He saved June and me from death in the worst flooding in the history of Hanalei Valley. My wife wasn't being dramatic: we really do owe him our lives."

"Capital, I say, capital!" Kingsley chirped. "Well done, Mr. Tana. You and Allen must tell me all about it at dinner."

"Please excuse me, I'm on duty." He escaped before anyone could protest, waves of emotion sweeping over him.

During the evening, John avoided contact with the woman he still loved. In his movement around the dining room he noted that the guests were delighted with the *coq au vin* that Joseph Still had created.

As they spooned in the dessert of honey-baked fruitcake, John stole a glance at Leinani's table. Their eyes locked. John's heart pulsed fast. He knew she wanted to speak to him.

A hubbub of noise filled the room as the guests of Princess Liliuokalani raved over the cake, demanding the chef. They stood, applauding. Still came from the kitchen blocking John's view. He escaped from the dining room and out into the alley. He stood, staring into the night, calming his beating heart.

After the guests of Liliuokalani left, John visited with Joe Still. They exchanged small talk about the evening, life on the island, and family. John felt a kinship with the man. They agreed to meet the following day to attend Still's church.

Chapter 40

"I hope you've been to a Catholic service before," Still said. "If you haven't, just follow my lead." The men ascended the steps of the Cathedral of Our Lady of Peace, entering through its massive doors. "Before today, I have not been to a Catholic mass, but I have been to this church." John smiled at the memory. "I brought a very holy man here, a kind and gentle man. In fact, I hope to visit him in Kalawao." John crossed himself as they entered the vestibule.

"You've met Father Damien?" Joe asked his eyes wide with surprise. "I'm sure he's a holy man, but he's also controversial." He suddenly turned and smiled. "Hello, Sister."

John saw a diminutive woman wearing the traditional habit of black, a white cowl draped over her head. She stared at John for a long moment. "You are Mr. Tana, are you not? It's nice to see you again, so many years since you were last here." Her eyes sparkled as she added, "And thank you again for your generous gift to the order and to Father De Veuster."

John tipped his head to acknowledge her thanks. "Father De Veuster is a wonderful man. I understand he's now at Kalawao, on Molokai."

The nun nodded and John informed her that he would be there soon, traveling with the princess. "Sister Maria, this is my friend, Joe Still, from Strasbourg."

The nun gave Still a slight nod and turned back to John. "Did I hear you say that you're off to Kalawao? If so, could you meet with me in the cloister after the service?" With that, Sister Maria made the sign of the cross over the two men and, clutching holy beads dangling from her neck, murmured prayers as she walked away.

After mass, John visited the nun, then invited Still to lunch at Ah Sam's. As the two men walked to Merchant Street, Still talked about his life before he settled in Hawaii. He told John that at the age of eighteen, he joined the French army to visit romantic places, but was instead thrust into the war between Prussia and France.

John listened with fascination as Joe described the French village of St. Privat, where Still was wounded three times, one of those wounds a saber cut into his chest requiring a lengthy hospitalization. He explained how, even though the French armies had surrendered, Paris held out for six months. "When an armistice was finally signed," he went on, "I was discharged back to Strasbourg, which by then had become part of Germany. My very good friend, Pierre La Follet, was forced to remain in the French army to fight the socialists who had taken over Paris."

John learned about war and a world so different from his own. Every description created an image in his head, a place he could only imagine. He learned how, upon Still's return home, everything had changed. A new German government had been installed in Strasbourg and it ordered that only German was to be spoken.

"They started a re-education program. All of us were expected to embrace German nationalism and their doctrine of *One People, One Reich.* I was lucky, because my family had a restaurant and I learned to cook there. It wasn't long, however, before more trouble started. The Germans began to draft all men ages eighteen to twenty-six."

The two men continued walking, John eager to hear more. "Please, go on with your story."

"I'm no coward. I fought bravely at St. Privat, but I'm French, not German. Why would I fight against my own country?" They slowed their pace to permit a horse-drawn cart to pass. "I decided to leave Strasbourg."

"Your problems were finally over?"

Joe smiled. "Not quite! Remaining French was easy, but I also knew that if I moved to France, I'd be re-drafted into the army."

John shook his head. "It looks like there was no way to come out ahead."

The men approached the restaurant and paused, looking at the town, the bustle of people moving about, doing business, and living their lives. They shared several minutes of a comfortable silence, the kind that only friends can share. When Joe spoke, his voice was low and filled with emotion.

"After what I've been through, I've come to the belief that war solves nothing. In fact, I'm opposed to war, which is why I decided to travel to America and start a new life."

John felt respect for his new friend, struggling with the idea of what courage it must take to leave a homeland, family and language, and strike out for places unknown.

"After living seven years in the States and hearing so much about Hawaii, I decided to try it. Besides," he added with a laugh, "it's even further away from the Kaiser."

They entered the Chinese restaurant and were joined by Still's friend, Abel Rodriguez. During the meal, Still said, "I heard you say that you gave part of your reward money to Father De Veuster and the Congregation of the Sacred Heart. Why would you, a non-Catholic, do that?"

John explained how he'd met the clergyman at the docks years ago and had been overwhelmed by the man's kindness. "His desire to do good things for others, without expecting any kind of reward, made me feel that he was Hawaiian. That's why I gave him the money."

Joe slapped his hand on the table. "Hear that, Rodriguez? Hawaiians give everything away. These people don't understand the meaning of property."

The Portuguese chewed on a toothpick, nodding. He withdrew it and speared a juicy piece of Chinese sausage. "Since I came here on the *Priscilla,* more than three years ago, I have found Hawaiian people very generous. Give you the shirt off their back." With a grin, he added, "But don't get them drunk, they can be mean."

John mulled over Joe's comment about Hawaiians giving everything away. "Why shouldn't I help the priest? I hadn't worked for the reward money. I only kept it to pay for Chin Sing's defense." John paused as he thought over the past. *He had wanted to use what was left to marry Leinani, but Ah Sam needed help to pay for his losses so he had given him part of the reward. Then she had decided to marry Kingsley.* "Why not give what was left to the Church to help the poor?" he challenged.

Before Joe could respond, Rodriguez announced, "That's a good thing to do, Mr. Tana, help the poor, that's the ticket to heaven. Tell me, where are you from and what kind of work do you do?"

John reached over for some fried wonton before answering. "I'm in the security business on Kauai. In a few days, I'll be escorting Princess Liliuokalani to the Molokai leper colony to provide her with protection."

Just then, Ah Sam arrived with a bowl of steaming egg-flower soup. "You go to Kalawao?" he asked, placing the bowl in the center of the table. "Place very sad, no like it." He looked at the strangers with John. "Hawaiians call it *The Grave Where One is Buried Alive.* Once you go, no come back." He dished out steaming soup, saving a bowl for himself.

"Leprosy," Joe mumbled. "The *mai pake,* the Chinese sickness."

"Not true!" Ah Sam insisted. "People call it mai pake because whites say we brought it here. Truth is, leprosy came with the foreign sailors."

"What I don't understand," John said, "is why people with leprosy are imprisoned in Kalawao. It's such a remote place, so bleak." He explained to the two men that it's a peninsula hemmed in by tall mountains. "The only sure way to get in is by sea. The government located the colony in a place where there's no safe harbor to land a boat."

It was Ah Sam who explained how the Hawaiian government first sent lepers to Kalawao. It was 1866 and they were caged in a ship anchored a hundred yards from the shore. "Sailors opened gates and push sick people into the water. Make them swim to the beach. Sailors throw food in barrels. Maybe stuff float to shore, maybe not, but the ship sail away and leave those people alone."

Intrigued by a story that had been suppressed for more than a decade, John asked, "But what happened to the lepers, once they swam ashore?"

"What do you think happen?" Ah Sam demanded his voice suddenly high in pitch. "People come on the beach, they find no house, no toilet, no plants to eat, nothing except what sailors throw from boat." His voice faltered for a moment, as if painful memories were surging up from a long-hidden place. Before anyone could speak, he continued, "I have Chinese friend, tell me it was survival of strongest. The biggest guys take what they want, rape women, and make weak ones into slaves. That's why Hawaiians call it 'a graveyard for the living'. The weak, sickly people have only dirt to eat until they die."

John cast his eyes onto the floor, his appetite suddenly gone. "I don't understand why these people were sent to Kalawao without food."

Joe placed a hand on John's arm. "Think about it. Why would the Christians who run the Board of Health want to spend money on sick Hawaiians? In their way of thinking, leprosy is God's punishment for living immoral lives and the wicked should pay for their sins."

Anger ran through John like an electric jolt. He shook his head to clear away the growing emotions. When he spoke, the words arrived through clenched teeth. "How can sick people help themselves if they have nothing? No tools, materials, seeds, nothing!"

"John, if you wanted to eradicate a group, what would you do? Feed them, care for them or—" Still paused for a dramatic moment, "—put them in a dungeon without food or water? Annihilation, that was the purpose of Kalawao. It took Father Damien, the man you call De Veuster, to help end that horror."

Rodriguez was quick to point out that the priest was the first foreign-born to travel to Molokai to help the lepers. There were many missionaries who could have made that trip—pilgrimage, truly—but lacked either the courage or the conviction.

"Rodriguez is right," Still agreed. "If the priest had not been Belgian, I'm not sure the foreign reporters would have descended on Hawaii to write his story. When they did, and reported on the despicable conditions, the Hawaiian Board of Health was humiliated. A Catholic priest showed more charity than the Calvinists."

The conversation shifted to lighter subjects until Sam returned with bowls of rice, spare ribs, pork hash, roast duck, lemon chicken and fried noodles. He spread the feast in the center of the table and then left for the kitchen, coming back with a large flagon of wine and four cups. As he poured it he said, "I think pretty soon Hawaiian be vanishing race." His comment caused several forks to stop mid-way.

"Why not?" Ah Sam continued. "Thousands die from disease, die imprisoned in Kalawao. I think more Hawaiians die than get born: big trouble for pure blood."

There was silence. Joe Still stood. "Let me propose a toast," he announced, raising his cup. "Thank you, Mr. Sam, for this delicious meal and good wine." He drank the last of it and remained standing. When no one spoke, he nodded and looked at each face. "Lest you doubt the real threat to the survival of the Hawaiians I suggest you study the meaning of Manifest Destiny."

John watched Rodriguez swirl the wine in his cup and wondered why this simple suggestion would cause the man to sneer. When the Portuguese began to speak, his voice was hard, challenging.

"Everybody knows about that," he insisted, waving away Joe's comment like a hat swatting at an insect. "Isn't that some new kind of religion that's supposed to take Hawaiians off to heaven, maybe even hell?" He finished with raucous bitter laughter that filled the room.

John turned at once to Joe Still. "Is that true?"

Joe sat down and shot Rodriguez an unpleasant glance. "No, Manifest Destiny is not a religion. It's a reason why government gains control of native land. If you travel across the United States like I did, you see very clearly what America has done to the Indians. With Manifest Destiny as their excuse, they finagled until they owned or stole all of the Indian land."

John sighed, wondering how this idea would be used against his own people.

"I learned plenty when I was a chef in the States," Joe added. He turned to Ah Sam. "You understand, right?"

Ah Sam nodded pensively. "Cook listens good when customers talk; we learn plenty."

"Exactly, and everywhere I went, I heard people saying the same thing: 'It's America's Manifest Destiny to master the Indians, and then move across the Pacific and colonize.' Let's face it, trade with Asia is big, and it's getting bigger."

Ah Sam poured the last of the wine and said, "Muk Fat has convinced my son that the best way for a Chinese to make money is through trade. My boy wants to open an import-export business."

"Gold has petered out in California," Joe said. "But there's new gold in Hawaii, and it's called sugar. Millions of dollars are to be made in Hawaiian sugar, which is why speculators are grabbing land and building sugar mills." He explained how, as chef, he overheard American businessmen and plantation owners talking about annexing the islands to the United States. "This treaty that Kalakaua made has created a dangerous economic tie between Hawaii and America and—"

John tensed so visibly that Joe fell silent. "Are you saying that this Manifest Destiny thing will cause the United States to take over our kingdom?"

Joe fixed his gaze on the stricken Hawaiian. "Look here, the treaty means big money to the sugar people and the merchants. They'll never let Hawaii escape from American clutches. Some of these men are ready to seize power now!"

John had heard rumors about the Honolulu business community funding a battalion of well-armed fighters, but no one could confirm it.

"They're called the Honolulu Rifles," Joe said, as if reading John's thoughts.

Rodriguez ran a hand across his bald head. "If they have men to fight and the desire to win, what's keeping them and America from taking over now? I mean, end the Hawaiian kingdom and finish off the Hawaiians?"

John looked expectantly at Still, the man who seemed to have a real grasp of the situation.

"If I had to guess," Joe replied, "I'd say it is the presence of British and French warships in the harbor. Those countries also have treaties with this kingdom and I believe they'd do their best to keep the Americans from claiming exclusive control over the port of Honolulu, Pearl Harbor, and the sugar."

When John bid goodbye to his new friends, his heart was heavy with worry. *I had acquired land and built a home and farm, yet if my property in Kahului could be easily taken, what would stop the sugar plantations from seizing my Kilauea land? If sick people could be thrown like garbage onto a god-forsaken peninsula and left to die, then what would happen if someone in my family became a leper? What if the monarchy was overthrown and America took control, who would protect the Hawaiian people? The sugar folks didn't care what happened to us.* Added to the sum of these worries was Mahealani, her belief in the power of the kahuna, her anger at him for choosing Christianity.

Chapter 41

On Monday, a messenger come to Ah Sam's requesting that John meet with Kingsley and Tucker at the Hawaiian Hotel for lunch. At first, he thought to reject it, but then he noticed a postscript from Leinani begging him to attend.

Dressed in his best clothes he arrived at the restaurant. He felt awkward to be standing waiting for the two men to arrive, but Still came from the kitchen, embraced him, and seated him at the best table in the dining room. He waited with John until the two businessmen arrived, and said, "I will make a special lunch for you, compliments of my friend." He patted John's shoulder then pulled seats out from the table.

"I didn't realize you were acquainted with the chef," Kingsley said.

John smiled, realizing that Still had given him a status greater than an ordinary policeman. "We have a mutual interest in religion and Manifest Destiny."

"How odd you should say that," Tucker commented. "I didn't realize that antiquated notion had spread to the islands."

"According to Still it is not an old idea, but a reality. If we start depending more on America for sugar prosperity, who knows what that country might do?"

"Hawaiians shouldn't trouble themselves with such trivialities." Kingsley's eyes narrowed as he uttered his remark.

"I don't think it's just idle talk," John answered with vehemence. "Our kingdom could be in danger."

"This onion soup is outstanding," Tucker interrupted, easing the rising tension. "John, your friend is an excellent chef. I can't wait to try his tips of beef with mushroom sauce."

"I agree with Allen. The food is excellent. But we didn't ask to have lunch with you, Mr. Tana, to discuss delightful eating. My wife tells me that you are accomplished in the martial arts. Tucker informs me that you own a private security business. You service sugar plantations on Kauai and do a fine job for them."

John shifted in his seat. It is not often that he heard such praise. "Thank you, Mr. Kingsley, for your compliments. What is it you wish to talk about?"

"Good. You are the kind of man I like, straight to the point. It's all about making money, Mr. Tana."

Tucker huddled over the table speaking in hushed tones, "It is about making money, but it isn't what you might be thinking." The businessman gave John a wink adding to the mystery of the meeting. John wondered what these men wanted. Is it legal?

Sensing that John might be confused, Kingsley's tone became conversational. "Most plantations in Hawaii are run on the Koloa model. Instead of paying workers with hard money or currency, script is issued."

John nodded his head. "Yes, I know about script. I used to be paid with those little pieces of cardboard with numbers written on them. You took your script to a store and you could buy what you wanted."

"Well done, Mr. Tana," Tucker patronized him. "We pay workers in script, gold, silver Spanish real, and the like. Recently King Kalakaua introduced currency to Hawaii."

Kingsley slapped the table jarring together dishes and silverware. Several luncheon guests looked in the direction of the clattering noise, returning to their meals once satisfied that what disturbed them had ended.

Kingsley glanced about to make sure there were no listeners, then said, "I apologize for my temper Mr. Tana, but we have counterfeiters in Hawaii. They are watering down our money. They are stealing our profits. They will ruin the economy. This theft must stop."

Before John could speak, Tucker raised his hand. "Besides phony money we have a big problem with opium use. Chinese workers are either absent from work or when they arrive are useless."

John let the revelations whirl around in his mind for some moments.

Theft, opium---these are hefty words. They smelled of danger.

The two businessmen fidgeted with their food as they waited for John's response.

"What does this have to do with me? Isn't this a problem for the police?"

Kingsley pursed his lips, raised his eyes to the ceiling, and then moved his face toward John. In hushed tones he said, "The Government claims they do not have the manpower to solve the problem. Possibly there are other reasons why they are unwilling to act. I don't know. But our merchants and plantations need help. That is why we are talking with you."

As he leaned forward, Tucker added, "I believe the answer to our problems lies in Chinatown.Kingsley's wife tells us that you have contacts within the Chinese community in Honolulu. Will you help us?"

Mildly surprised by the question, yet pleased that these men would seek his help, John did not immediately answer. *He thought of Leinani's father, a sugar plantation owner who had seized his land and ordered his death. The business community in Honolulu had never helped him, especially during the trial of Chin Sing. Even today, despite their need, Kingsley and Tucker met him at a hotel restaurant. He is not invited to their homes or offices. He wondered if Leinani wanted him to help her husband. He had a suspicion she had asked the two men to request his aid.*

"All right gentlemen, I will do what I can to help you. We need to talk about terms and conditions of the job and I need to get as much information from you as I can."

Kingsley and Tucker explained that the center of the counterfeiting and opium smuggling operation is in Chinatown. Beyond that conviction, they had nothing to offer. John asked the two men to request that Kilauea plantation extend his leave and gave them several messages for his employees on Kauai.

After lunch John went to the harbor seeking Aaloa. When he asked about his friend he discovered that the bone crusher had become the head of the Stevedore's Union.

"Nothing comes in and out of Honolulu without us guys knowing about it," Aaloa bragged. "Maybe sixty days ago we off-loaded crates of furniture and other stuff from this boat from China. They went to an address just off King Street. Then the boys unloaded some other big boxes. They had air holes in them. We take them Maunakea Street. Us guys think maybe China people in the crates. Could be women? Could be something else?"

At Ah Sam's restaurant that evening, John learned other interesting information. Opium could be purchased on the hush-hush from an herbalist doing business on Maunakea Street. Ah Sam's son, Choi Waihoku, had friends who lived on Maunakea Street so John gave the fourteen-year-old an assignment.

Later that evening John wandered over to the Whaler's Bistro to visit a friend. "Eh, brah, how you been? What you up to?" Daniel Noa asked. He gave John a friendly jab in the ribs. Noa leaned over and whispered, "You want to get laid tonight? I know a new place on Maunakea Street. Some good stuff there. Take you to the moon, brah."

Chapter 42

Two days later a fat, bearded, Hawaiian with a beige gunnysack slipped over his head slowly walked on King Street. The tired old man turned onto Maunakea. Dangling above the street were dozens of rectangular banners with Chinese writing. Fastened onto brown wood-frame buildings were round red and yellow lanterns with similar symbols covering their notched sides. There were several two-story buildings on the street. Some had balconies protected by bamboo railings.

Attached to many of the structures were awnings held up by poles stuck into the earth. Beneath these yellow-brown coverings were tables displaying goods for sale. Hanging from the supports were roasted ducks, their dark brown bodies gleaming with oily, sugared syrup. Scores of Chinese men and a few women shopped along the roadway.

Tapping a six-foot wooden staff on the hard earth surface of the street, the fat Hawaiian limped to a stool at an outdoor café. Easing his body onto the armless seat, he ordered tea and sweet dumplings. His eyes, hidden by the shadow of his broad-brimmed hat, searched the roadway.

On the opposite side stood a two-story building, the front windows partially covered with curtains. Jars of herbs along with scales and other measuring instruments were displayed. Entry was through a bright red door. Above it hung a Chinese sign. At each end, lanterns with symbols were hung. Like other buildings it had a second-story balcony with bamboo rails.

On this upper platform, a dark-clothed man smoked a rolled cigarette, his eyes slowly swiveling along the street. For a moment, the guard's gaze rested upon the fat Hawaiian with his staff leaning against the café wall. Then his watchful eyes moved along the roadway.

To the right side of the building there was a narrow alleyway, slightly wider than the corpulent body of the Hawaiian. A thin stream of water flowed along it and emptied into the street. From time to time Chinese men sloshed along the mud of the narrow path and entered the red door.

His meal finished, the old Hawaiian attempted to rise from his stool. The guard on the second story watched with amusement as the fat man forced himself erect using his staff. He laughed when the elder stumbled into the street, almost falling on his face. For minutes, the old one stood in the roadway. With a sneer, the second-story guard flicked his cigarette at him, then turned away. Slowly the old man waddled down the street to the harbor.

Chapter 43

Three days later, John outlined his plan to Kaipo, Kunani, and Aaloa. "The Chinese hui that is conducting illegal business in Honolulu is housed in a long rectangular building fronting onto Maunakea Street. In the rear, there is a narrow courtyard and a one-story building."

"Yeah, I know the place," Aaloa said. "It shares a common wall with a business next to it that faces the mountains. On the ocean side, there's a long alley that runs to Smith."

John took out a pencil and paper. He drew a diagram on it as a bird might look down into the building if the roof had been lifted from it.

Pointing with his pencil to the front of the structure, John said, "This is an apothecary shop. It sells Chinese herbs and other medicine. But it's only a front for what is happening inside."

As he studied the map, Aaloa grunted and ran his palm around his wiry beard. "I think there is a back door in the alley behind the building. Does the front door of the shop lead down a hallway to the rear door?"

"Right," John answered, pointing to a line in his diagram. "This is the back wall of the apothecary shop. There is a doorway that opens to the hallway leading to the rear exit."

"What's behind the apothecary shop?" Kunani waved a finger at the rectangular space between the apothecary wall and the back end.

John drew more lines on his diagram. "When you step through the apothecary door, to your left is a stairway leading to the outside balcony in front of the building and a second floor. Along its hallway are a half-dozen bedrooms."

"I bet you're going to tell us that you can get laid in one of those rooms," Aaloa sniggered, making gestures with his hands.

"You know a lot about this place," Kaipo challenged the bone breaker. "You been a customer at this cat house?"

Aaloa gave Kaipo a friendly slap on his head. "Maybe you better ask John that question. He seems to know what goes on inside. Hey, brah, what's it like, that Asian stuff? Some good, eh?" Aaloa winked broadly.

John ignored the accusation and answered Kunani's question, "Aaloa and Kaipo are right. In the bedrooms on the second floor you can be entertained by Chinese prostitutes illegally shipped to Hawaii. Pay a fee to the merchant in the apothecary shop and you'll be assigned a room and a girl."

"Okay, now that we know what's upstairs, what's downstairs?" Kaipo asked. "Eh, brother John, you never answered Aaloa's question. How is that Chinese stuff?"

"Never tried it and don't ever intend to. What I know about the place comes from a friend. Ask him how he enjoys the Chinese stuff. Don't ask me." John dismissed the jibes with a wave of his hand.

"Okay, okay, don't get irritated," Aaloa soothed. "But you certainly know a lot about the inside."

"I have our friend Jimmy Noa to thank and a fourteen-year old boy."

"Did you send a kid into a cat house?" Kaipo grimaced in mock horror.

John delivered a soft punch to his employee's arm. "No way."

Aaloa studied the crude drawing. "What's on the first floor?"

John drew more lines on the diagram. "Behind the apothecary shop, there are two large rooms. One room is near the shop. That is where gambling, opium sales, and opium smoking occurs."

With a pudgy finger Aaloa pointed to a line bisecting the downstairs hallway. "What's this line? A wall? A door?"

"That is a wall with a locked door closing off the hallway to a rear room. I don't know what's in that room but my guess is that is where the counterfeiting is happening."

"All right, boss man," Kunani teased. "Now that we know the layout, what's the plan?"

John huddled over the map, moving a hand along the diagram. "There are three guards watching the place. One is in the apothecary shop and screens incoming customers. Another is on the balcony. He watches the street and patrols along the second-floor platform. A third is stationed in the courtyard. We hit the place in the late afternoon when the counterfeiting will be at its height and the other action will be getting underway."

Chapter 44

A muscular Hawaiian opened the red door of the apothecary shop. Alarm bells tinkled, warning those inside of his entry. A sharp smell of dead roots and dried leaves momentarily overpowered the intruder.

Behind a counter stood a thinly-bearded Chinese man, who stared at John through delicate, golden-rimmed glasses. Dressed in jasmine-colored Mandarin pajamas, the Chinese asked, "What kanaka want?" As he spoke, the stringy white hair descending from his chin bounced against a golden medallion hanging from his neck.

Without hesitation John answered, "Woman!"

"No woman here," the apothecary protested.

"*Zao zuo ai, gan, cao, cao.*" John spoke in Chinese saying to the druggist that he came to the shop to be satisfied by a woman.

A squat, heavy-set man detached himself from a stool at the door. "Kanaka want *gan*? You have money?" John showed him several gold real, and gave one as a gift to the pimp.

"Okay, kanaka, you a little early for fun, but give me two dallah." The pimp held out his hand for the money.

John placed two gold coins on his palm.

"Okay, go in this door, upstairs, room number three."

John climbed the stairs, walking along the inside balcony to room three. He paused, took off his shoes and padded back along the second floor to the outside balcony door. Opening it, he motioned to the guard, "Come quick. Woman is very sick."

When the guard passed by, John hit him with a small club. The man went to his knees and John hit him a second time. He dropped unconscious to the floor of the hallway. John dragged the inert body to an alcove and tied him up.

John stole along the upstairs balcony. He could see the length of the hallway below. John had just wormed his way past number four when, with a "thwack", its door opened. Sharp words were exchanged between a person outside the door and someone inside the room.

A woman's voice cooed, "*Nimen gan gua ma*?"

John huddled against the wall. Below, he heard three sharp raps on the rear door. A voice spoke Chinese. The rear door opened. The Chinese speaker exited into the courtyard.

At bedroom four a Chinese man continued to stand looking inside the room. John held his breath, his body partially hidden from view by the open door. If the unhappy customer turned toward him John knew he would be seen.

"*Zao zuo ai? Cao*!" the irate patron shouted.

John smiled. The two people were insulting each other. Describing how unsatisfactory their coupling had been.

Come on, John thought. *Get out of here. Would the noise bring the pimp upstairs? How long would he wait before checking on him? He figured that he had twenty minutes at most. Ten of those minutes had been used up.*

With a final, "*Cao*!" the irate customer walked along the balcony to the front stairway. As soon as the man made his descent, John moved. Bending low, he padded to the rear stairs which were narrow and without a protective side rail.

Luck held. No one discovered him. John rapped on the rear door three times mumbling something that sounded Chinese.

A stocky man dressed in black opened the door. John struck him with a combination of vicious blows. He thrust extended fingers of his right hand into the man's navel, followed by a powerful right cross to the lower jaw. The Chinese sagged to the dirt of the courtyard. John made certain that he stayed asleep with a rap against the side of his head.

Using the inert body of the guard to prop open the door, John stepped into the courtyard. He gave a birdcall signal.

Sliding along the alleyway Aaloa, Kaipo, and Kunani joined John. Following John's plan, Kaipo climbed to the second floor. Kunani stood guard in the hallway by the rear door.

John and Aaloa sidled to the door of the second room on the ground floor. Through the thin wood came the clicking of a turning wheel. Chinese voices mingled with the monotonous sound of a machine.

John gave Aaloa a signal. Together the two men crumbled the door into jagged splinters blowing it from its hinges. Inside, a slender Chinese stood in pajamas grinding a printing press. By a table, another man poured liquid metal into molds.

The man at the printing press seized a long knife. He assumed a fighting stance, left hand thrust outward with palm open, right hand behind him with the knife ready to spear John.

Aaloa's opponent threw molten metal at him, but in his hurry, burnt himself. The bone breaker crashed a chair over his head, ending his cries and reducing him to an unconscious heap on the floor.

In the cluttered room, John's opponent could not use his feet to strike. He waited for the Hawaiian to make a move.

John feinted to the left. The man stabbed with the knife. John dodged the thrust.

Again, John feinted, this time to the right side. His opponent charged with short, sliding steps trying to strike John's neck with his hand. The blow missed.

John stepped from side-to-side, confusing his opponent. With a loud, "hayah" the counterfeiter charged, extending his knife hand outward in a thrust at John's belly.

With a sweep of his arm, John brushed the knife away and smashed his right hand onto the bridge of the man's nose. Blood spurted onto the two men. John held onto the knife arm and struck several blows with his fist. The weapon fell to the floor as the Chinese collapsed.

"Eh, John, what took you so long to put your guy to sleep? My guy, he went to bed an hour ago. Messy, messy, you red all over. Look at me. Clean," Aaloa needled his friend, a wide grin on his face.

A rattling of the center hall door ended further joking. Aaloa removed his nightstick and rushed to the threshold of the counterfeiting room just as the pimp appeared with a knife in his hand. Aaloa thrust his long stick into his stomach. The man lost his lunch. Aaloa grabbed him by his pajama collar and clubbed him across the back of his head. The fight ended.

From the gambling room, several men emerged into the hallway. John called out, “We are deputized Hawaiian policemen. You are under arrest. Line up against the side wall.”

One man started to comply, but three others lit out through the front door into Maunakea Street. The complying man hesitated, then turned and followed his fleeing friends.

From the open door of the gambling room waves of pungent sweet smoke fumed into the hallway. John looked inside. There were several tables strewn with gambling equipment. On the far wall, John saw bunks. Inert bodies lay on the wooden beds.

Chapter 45

"Marvelous work, Mr. Tana. You have shut down a counterfeiting operation, seized thousands of ounces of unlicensed opium, and freed a half-dozen teen-aged Chinese girls. The city of Honolulu, the business community, the sugar plantations are in your debt. Will you remain with us in Honolulu and open a security business?" Kingsley asked.

"I agree with everything Jim said. I know we can offer you some very lucrative work. As we prosper, you will prosper," Tucker added.

John thought of the offer for several moments before answering. "I will think about what you suggest and let you know my decision when I return from Molokai."

"What venture are you undertaking?" Kingsley asked.

"The princess is visiting the lepers at the colony. I'm providing security for her. Gentlemen, excuse me. I have a date to visit with my Aunt Malia in the home you gave her, Mr. Kingsley." John left the two businessmen.

Painful memories arose in him as he walked Waikiki Road. When he came to the white picket fence surrounding Malia's cottage he could not go in. John turned to leave, emotions of anger, hate, lost love whirled inside him. He stopped.

He would not run like some beaten cur. Twelve years had passed since Auntie had uttered her sad words that a Hawaiian man has nothing. By any standard of judgment, he is successful. He had land, money, two paying jobs, and a family.

John opened the gate, stepped to the front door and knocked.

"Hey, John, no stand outside, come in."

Malia sat in her parlor. Age had not marred her skin. Her face and eyes were clear, bright, and focused on him. A sweet smile curled her lips. John kissed the old woman's forehead. Pointing to her dining table she said, "Go eat. Plenty dry squid, fish. Poi on the sink."

Except for the squid, John declined other food. As he tore into a salted tentacle he asked, "How's the family?"

Malia sighed, shaking her head. "David drink too much. Go with bad women. He has no money, no job. So, what he do? He steal. He get caught after he almost kill somebody. He lucky he no hang. David in prison." Auntie breathed heavily as she fought her tears but her control over her feelings evaporated, and she rocked in her chair crying.

There was silence in the room broken only by the low noise of crackling lauhala floor matting squished by the curved wood of Malia's rocking chair. John chewed on his salted morsel waiting for his aunt to speak.

She stirred herself from her sadness and said, "The Makanani taro fields are no more. If you no can pay for lease, you out! Chinese take over. Plant rice where taro once grew. They have duck farms all over Waikiki. They sure like those stink eggs." Auntie laughed at her little joke.

Outside the cottage, carriage wheels crunched to a stop. The gate to the picket fence squeaked open. A radiant Leinani burst into the parlor.

She ran to John by the sink. As he stood still, Leinani threw herself into his arms, pressing her body into him, kissing him with a fervor that overwhelmed him.

As the room crackled around his head, Leinani pulled away. Her eyes fell to the floor as she withdrew to a more respectable distance.

Leinani lifted her face, brushing tears from her eyes. "I am so happy you helped my husband. He told me you would be here. You have no idea how much he praises you. Thank you, thank you for what you have done."

John spent the afternoon learning of Leinani's new life: two children, a boy and girl, a mansion, servants, and luxuries. James Kingsley is generous and loves her very much.

Robert Grant has adopted her into his family and made her his sole heir. She lacks for nothing except social acceptance. To the wives of the missionaries and other Americans she is a half-blood and must be kept in her place. Up to now she has not been allowed to move out of the prison of her caste.

John's bravery and resourcefulness in capturing the counterfeiters is the talk of the community. Allen and June Tucker have related wondrous stories of their rescue from the Hanalei flood. Overnight, John is a heroic figure. Leinani has let it be known that they are relatives. John's celebrity status has produced a thaw in the attitude of the women of New England. Leinani is now acceptable.

As she said this, John thought he understood her enthusiastic greeting. *Yet as she continued to speak, he felt there were other things she wanted to say. He could see in her eyes a hidden emotion.*

John shared his new life with her. His marriage, two children, and the land he had bought and cultivated. She sighed many times as he related his story. *He wondered if she regretted her decision to marry Kingsley.*

When it came time to leave, she kissed him with the same passion as when she first entered. The hydra of love swelled within him, the memory of her nakedness in Shaw's cabin rose in his mind. It threatened to overcome his resolve to keep their relationship beyond reproach.

"Hey, you two," Malia whispered. "Time for John to go home."

With a shudder, Leilani broke away, tears in her eyes. John heard her sob, "But for Maria." *He knew why he had lost her.*

"Goodbye to you both," he said and fled. *John ran along the roadway, half hoping Leinani would pursue him. When he dwelt upon that thought, he ran faster, realizing there could be no turning back.*

Exhausted, he arrived at his temporary residence at the home of Joe Still. The chef had returned from work. He asked no questions about John's obvious distress. Long into the night the two men talked of the future. Finally, a promise was extracted from Still to move to Kauai.

Chapter 46

With a loud whistle, the steamship *Likelike* eased into the quay at Honolulu Harbor. Robert Grant searched the platform for a servant who would convey him home. Instead, he saw his wife, Sheila, who waved at him with a pink, lacey handkerchief.

Perplexed, Grant waited anxiously for the exit bridge to be emplaced. Once it was fixed, he stalked down the fenced plank and onto the wharf. Sheila rushed to him, planted a kiss, and before her husband could speak said, "I came because I have terrible news for you."

"What could be so urgent? What is this news?"

"Your trollop of a daughter and son-in-law have made a hero of your enemy."

"Shelia, I wish you would be more respectful of Leinani. She is not a street walker and you shouldn't continually insult her as you often do."

"It's only because you are blind as to what these Hawaiian women are like. They will sleep with anyone. Just look at our king and his Snuggery or Nuggery or whatever he calls it. Hula dancing all day long, drinking wagons of champagne, and the illicit game kilu he plays at night."

"I have no excuses for Kalakaua, he is an immoral sot. But Leinani is not of that kind. She is a refined lady. Kingsley is satisfied she was a virgin when they married. There was blood on the sheets. That is all I really care about."

"You men are so naïve, so blind. A woman needs just one thing: pig's blood in a vial, sprinkle it on the sheets, and *voila* she lost her maidenhood on her wedding night."

"This debate is pointless. What is this startling news?"

"Your daughter and son-in-law have made a folk hero out of that boy, John Tana."

"What! How did they do that?"

"The police were not doing their job to eliminate counterfeiting. Leinani connived to get James to hire the trouble maker. He wound up not only capturing the Chinese making the bogus bills, but also cracking a teen-aged whorehouse, and an opium den."

"Damnation! That's why you called him a hero."

"That's not all. Kingsley, with his friend Tucker, are promoting him to be head of security for all the plantations."

"Never will I allow this to happen. Stop at Leinani's home. I would have a word with her."

But at the residence, the servants reported she was at Queen's hospital doing charity work. Mr. Kingsley could be found at his downtown office.

Leaving Sheila at home Grant headed for the heart of Honolulu. But Kingsley was at lunch. Grant left word to meet in his office on an urgent matter and left.

Settling into a dark red chair in his chambers, Grant laid out the newspapers on his koa desk. The walls of the room were also lined with the same rich brown wood. An expensive oriental rug covered the floor. The whole aspect of the room displayed great wealth.

From the news reports, the king had been issuing paper currency which could be easily duplicated. Counterfeit bills had been showing up at merchandise stores. Even silver coins that carried Kalakaua's image were suspect of being less than genuine. The police had been impotent to deal with the problem. One reporter suggested they were bribed to look the other way.

Plantations were finding that their employees were often too drugged to come to work. While alcohol ruined the Hawaiian as a worker, illegal opium harmed the Chinese worker. Sugar planters complained, and the authorities did nothing.

In this economic crisis in Honolulu, two businessmen, Kingsley and Tucker, had engaged a pure Hawaiian security officer from Kauai. Within five days, John Tana had smashed the crime ring. To the delight of the church people of Oahu he also closed a vice operation of teen-aged prostitutes. James Kingsley said of these accomplishments, "We are in great debt to this man. Once he returns from his mission to Molokai the business community will offer him work as a private security agency for Oahu sugar plantations."

Fuming, Grant set aside the newspapers and shouted to an empty room, "Never will that rotten kanaka be given work by white men."

Shaken by what he had read, Grant reached for his cigars, lit one without clipping it, filled his lungs with the aromatic weed, and blew out towers of smoke. Agitated, he stood up and paced the room deciding what to do.

A knock at the door, his clerk popped in and said, "Mr. Kingsley is here."

Grant nodded, and began folding papers on his desk. When Kingsley came in he showed him the quote from the paper. "Are you seriously considering offering this man a business on this island?"

Flustered by the accusation, Kingsley drew back. In a defensive tone he said, "Why not? The man did us a huge favor. He didn't ask for money, just did the work without pay. The results were extraordinary. Even the king is grateful for having saved the value of his new currency."

"You don't know him like I do. He burnt all my buildings in Kahalui. He went to Lahaina and waylaid three sailors, maiming them. Then he took on my supervisor Gonzales, broke his leg. Later, he killed him. He ran an illegal still in Honolulu, caused the death of one man, and injured several policemen. To top off all these acts of mayhem, he and his friends beat up half a dozen sailors in the harbor. There is more, but close to home, he raped a French woman who was a dear friend of your wife. Except for my vigilance he might have raped Leinani as well. You are dealing with a bad man."

"I had no idea he was so vicious. Leinani praised him highly. Tucker and his wife vouched for him. He saved them both from a terrible flood. She even kissed him, called him 'Lothario'."

"You see, that is how this man operates. Ingratiates himself with the men, and seduces their wives. Keep a sharp eye on my daughter. I intend to have a word with her."

"You have made me very worried. Leinani has said nothing but good things about this man. She even asked to invite him to our home. In our meetings he seemed so presentable, so friendly. He did not ask for money."

"You know the old saying, 'you can't judge a book by its cover.' This Hawaiian has buffaloed your wife, and found a way to fool people on Kauai. I would wager he is guilty of many crimes on that island. I will not let you sully the reputation of this family by helping him in any way."

"What are we to do? What explanations can I give the news media for all the praises and promises of reward I have heaped upon him?"

Grant drew smoke from the stub of his cigar. Its smoldering end dropped ash onto the carpet. Irritated by his negligence he strode to the door and summoned his clerk to clean up the mess. While the servant worked he returned his attention to Kingsley. "One thing for certain we must do: forbid your wife to see or speak of this knave again. Don't mention any of the sordid matters I have related to you. There will be only distortions and denials on her part. Let me have a word or two with her before you make any demands. As to our next step, I will arrange a poker game with our influential friends. Leave it to me to remedy this situation."

Finished with his cleaning the clerk rose from the floor. Grant placed a hand on his arm. "Go to Wailuku Plantation. Gunter is to report here to me three days hence."

The servant left, followed by Kingsley. Grant went to his desk and pulled out a long-barreled .44 caliber Colt revolver. He rubbed his hands across the shining metal. He grasped the pearl handles in his fist, aimed the weapon at the corner of the room, and slowly pulled the trigger. The hammer clicked, falling onto an empty chamber. From the same drawer, he pulled out a full box of ammunition. He shook the container. "Enough bullets to kill a dozen John Tanas," he muttered. Then he smiled as he spun the empty cylinder several times, mimicking the sound of a roulette wheel. *With this weapon, Gunter could not possibly fail, he thought.*

Chapter 47

Molokai

Sea spray splashed onto the deck of the coastal steamer chugging toward the island of Molokai. Horses whinnied, fighting the restraints that held them tied to the main rail of the ship. In the half-light of early morning John stared at the slot of sea between Lanai and Molokai. *He thought of Leinani, remembering her nude body being washed by the tiny waterfall on the beach of the 'island of the ghosts'. He recalled his fear when Shaw pursued them. Fear that the captain would recapture her and she would be gone forever.*

A pod of dolphins raced to the ship. John watched them keep pace with the steamer, frolicking like children, making constant graceful dives into the churning water, mimicking the up and down plunging of the boat. They were friendly animals, chirping as they swam through the sea. *John wondered if they were the last happy sight the lepers had as their boat steamed toward the foreboding peninsula that would serve as a prison until death.*

In the distance, John saw the dark mountains hemming in the leper colony, a mantle of black clouds hovering over them like the wild hair of a witch. In the dim light, he likened the sheer cliffs to a great skull that fell with sightless eyes into the sea. *He imagined the peninsula of Kalaupapa as a tongue sticking out from its jaws preparing to draw into its maw victims to be devoured.*

The voices of retainers of the princess coming from the innards of the steamer woke him from his imaginations. It was time to begin preparations for the princess and her retinue to disembark. He must perform his duties.

The water turned from ink to a lighter blue as the sun burst through the clouds flinging amber light onto the land. Ahead of the boat, waves washed onto mounds of dark rocks that fringed the shore. A ship attempting to land would be smashed onto the stones. Now John understood why the lepers were poked from their cages into the open sea. Their provisions in barrels were also thrown overboard. Sick people and their supplies floated onto the jagged rocks of the peninsula as their transport sailed away. It was after they landed that the true horror of the abandonment began.

The engine noise stopped. The steamer slid into an anchorage seventy-five yards from shore.

"Easy with those boxes, let's not drop them in the water," John scolded as he supervised the off-loading of equipment, supplies, and gifts. Everything was brought for the lepers and he was determined that nothing would be lost.

Worry lined his face and he appeared older than a few weeks ago. Just a half-hour earlier, the princess had decided to go ashore with some of her retinue without waiting for him. When he questioned this, she declared, "What do I have to fear? These are my loyal subjects!" And then he watched her being helped into the boat by her retainers, and the entire company rowed to shore. John saw a ragtag group of lepers awaiting the princess, and his stomach churned with worry.

John's concern proved groundless. She was met on the beach by Father Damien, the resident Protestant minister, and the colony supervisor. Those lepers who joined in the welcome treated her respectfully, and they moved as one large group to the Protestant church.

John finished overseeing the freight transfer and took the boat to the landing place. He was struck by the starkness of the peninsula, the sparse growth, small clumps of shrubs, and the few trees that managed to thrust themselves above the rock-strewn earth.

Some distance from shore, there were small white bungalows, shacks, and shanties that marched in an uneven line across the headland. Visible from where he stood were two churches, one for the Protestant lepers, and the other for the Catholics.

During John's stay, he learned about leprosy and its victims. There were lepers with obvious signs, often with hideously bulbous faces, reddish skin, and fingers in a state of decay. When the extremities lost all sensation because the nerves failed to function, toes and fingers were amputated or fell off. Some of the lepers were so terribly afflicted with corporal decay that their bodies were infested with worms.

What John found fascinating were those who appeared unblemished. He learned that some of these people were in the very early stages of the disease. Others were not lepers at all, but *kokua*, the true saints of the settlement, men and women who had volunteered to live in this island prison because a husband, wife, child, or parent had been sentenced to a life of isolation. The kokua provided loving care, many of them oblivious to the dangers of infection.

At the church service, John watched eight hundred subjects pay tribute to their princess. The leper choirs of Kalawao filled the sanctuary with hymns of hope and devotion. He saw how their songs, their respectful attitude, and even their good wishes overwhelmed Liliuokalani. When the service was complete, she declared, "On my return to Honolulu, I will do what is necessary to make Father Damien a Knight Commander of the Royal Order of King Kalakaua." John wondered if such a grand gesture was enough.

During a long pause in the ceremonies, John sought out the Catholic priest. The man's round, clean-shaven face lit up with delight when he delivered boxes of gifts and a letter from Sister Maria. So moved was the cleric that he took John's hand into his and held it. Through thick, bushy eyebrows, the man's eyes smiled. "It has been many years since we last met." The wind tousled his curly hair and gave him a rakish look. As if sensing this, he laughed and pushed his broad-brimmed black hat onto his head.

John refused the priest's offer of help with the boxes and followed the man along a path leading to a small cottage. "These are gifts from people in Honolulu, and from countries around the world. You do know that you're considered a saint by many of them."

"No, no, I'm not that at all. I am here to do God's work for those who are sick." Damien stopped at the little house and held open the door. "Please, come into my home."

John waved the priest in and entered after him, noting that the man hobbled. It was soon evident that he suffered terrible pain in his feet, and John felt helpless to ease his trouble.

Inside were two Hawaiian women. Damien sent them to watch the children who were using the graveyard as a playground. "My sisters of charity, they do housework and cook for me, but most important they help me care for the orphan children whose parents have died here."

Father Damien settled himself into a chair, wincing as he shifted his feet. He offered a plain, rough, wood stool to John. "Would you like some water?" he asked, and apologized for not having more to offer. "As you see, I lead a simple life." When John required nothing, he asked, "So what news do you bring me?"

John set to unloading the boxes, placing each item on a plank table resting on saw horses. When the boxes were empty, he reached into the pouch attached to his belt. "I believe that this is important. Sister Maria warned me that trouble is coming here, to Kalawao." To convey the seriousness of what he was about to say, John pulled the stool closer and sat down, his knees nearly touching the priest's. As if comprehending the urgency in this, Damien leaned closer.

"Father Albert Montiton will soon be arriving at the colony."

"Father Albert?" repeated the priest, his eyes widening in confusion.

"For some reason, he's convinced that you've violated your oath of chastity." It pained John to reveal these allegations, yet he felt it was kinder than to learn them from a letter. "There are rumors about your having relations with a woman and he intends to have it out with you and secure your confession to sin."

Damien shook his head, as if clearing out something bothersome and alien. "But I've done nothing to justify such an accusation." Suddenly, he sat straighter. "Let him come. I have a clear conscience with nothing to hide." And then he rose from the table, wincing. "Gout." He shuffled to a desk in the corner of the room. From it he removed a locket and then, taking a pen, jotted something on a tiny piece of paper. He folded the message and placed it inside the case of gold. That done, he shuffled back to his chair.

"Thank you, John Tana, for what you have brought me, and for the money you have given to our order. I have heard your story of your stillborn son and the sadness it has caused." With that, he held out his hand. "This is holy jewelry. Within it I have placed a prayer asking the Virgin Mary to heal your wife. To give comfort to both of you, I will pray for the soul of your son that he may find eternal peace." He handed the gift to John, and closed his eyes, lips moving.

After a long and comforting silence, Damien made the sign of the cross. "May heaven bless you, in the name of the Father, Son, and the Holy Spirit."

John smiled at this gentle man and stood. "You are very kind. Thank you, it will be a comfort to my wife. Forgive me, I must go and perform my duties."

When the priest moved to rise, John held up a hand. The man settled back down, gratitude on his face. "Farewell, John Tana. Go with God."

He clutched the locket and walked out of the priest's house. There was nothing in his heart or mind that could convince him that Damien was immoral. As he strode away, the smell of death from the adjacent graveyard breathed over him. *It made him shiver and reminded him that here, on this barren peninsula, his people were dying.*

Chapter 48

Honolulu

Grant climbed the steps of the Kingsley mansion. Along each side of the imported marble grew stalks of red flowers with stems of broad green leaves thrusting upward beside them. This exotic hedge ringed the great house giving it an opulent, oriental look. The broad veranda he stepped onto was guarded by a long, white, wooden fence which matched the color of the house. Deep brown trim framed the windows and entry door.

He grasped the large brass knocker and struck it firmly against the metal plate. He repeated the summons a second time. Steps came to the door, it opened a crack and Grant pushed the servant aside, entering the cool hallway of the residence. "Where is my daughter?"

"In the sewing room."

"Fetch her."

Grant stepped into a drawing room. For some moments, he stared at the simple but elegant furniture as if he hadn't seen it before. *Should I stand or seat myself? He decided to stand. Where? The mantelpiece, that's the spot and I'll arrange a chair facing me. That way I could look down upon her like a judge.*

With an arm casually draped over a shelf he watched his daughter enter the room. Her hazel eyes brightened with happiness, and she rushed to him. "Oh, Father, I'm glad you came. You have been gone so long." With that outburst, she gave him a kiss on the cheek and clasped him to her bosom.

With the expression of love, Grant's stern resolve to lecture collapsed in disarray. Leinani drew back. "Though I am happy to see you, it's unusual for you to come in the middle of the day. It's not bad news that you bring?" A worried expression crossed her face.

"No, it's nothing like that. What…what were you doing?" Grant stammered as he sought time to recover from the emotions that surged within him.

"I've been making dressing gowns for patients at the hospital."

"For pay?"

"Oh, no, I volunteer my time and I use my own money to get the supplies I need for the poor sick folks."

"You do this without charge!"

"Oh, yes. My reward is the happiness I see on people's faces when I have nursed them back to health. Families appreciate what I am doing to make their loved ones well."

Incredulous, Grant said with vehemence, "You touch those that are ill and breathe their foul corruption!"

"Oh yes—"

"Why?"

"Of all the graces, 'faith, hope, and charity; the greatest of these is charity'. This is from the Bible. You and my husband have provided me with all that I need. I cannot spend my time in idleness like other women do. I must give what I can to others. Nursing is my fulfilment of God's command to do charity."

Her words struck Grant like a thunderbolt. So much of his life had been spent in taking, not giving. His only child had a virtue that he lacked. For many moments, he stood silent. His hand smoothed his hair, palmed his face, and wiped the sudden sweat from his brow. *At fifty could he possibly move away from the unscrupulous pursuit of money? Maybe not, but his daughter might be his way to salvation? He knew with a certainty why he loved her. Leinani had a goodness which he did not have.*

"Father, you are so quiet, did I say something wrong?"

He clasped her hands. "No, you did not. You have said something that I would like to be, but find it is too late in life for me to change. As you do your good works pray for me."

"I always do. But is this just a friendly visit or is there something important you wish to talk about? Let me see. The children are in excellent health and doing outstanding in school. I am well, happy doing my charitable work, and very content in my marriage. James provides me with all I need. Does that answer all your concerns?"

Grant felt suddenly defensive. He no longer controlled their meeting. In a deep voice he said, "We need to discuss a delicate matter, John Tana."

"Isn't he wonderful? With his masterful sleuthing he solved a mountain of social problems for me. I told him so. Are you going to offer him a security job?"

"You have seen him recently!"

Leilani blushed, dropped her eyes, and for a moment she felt panic. Had word of her happiness when she met John reached her father? "Yes."

Grant saw his opportunity. "Were you unfaithful?"

Leinani reared back. "How can you say that? I visited Aunt Malia, John was there. We exchanged our histories. He is married with two children. He has a large farm at a place called Koolau near the Kilauea River. My cousin has several successful businesses on Kauai."

"I apologize for being blunt. I couldn't help remembering the past when he constantly pestered you. I knew then as I know now that Kingsley is the right man for you. As your father, I feel I must protect your good name." He reached his hands to her shoulders, pulled her to him and kissed her forehead.

"It's your good character I came to talk about. You know from the past how he abused your friend Maria. I think there may still be a warrant outstanding for rape of your teen-aged schoolmate. On my part, I have listed him as a suspect in the brutal murder of my employee, Gonzalez. These are facts which the Honolulu business community have not been made aware of and could sully your character if you continue to support him."

Leinani shook her head. "I understand your concern. John's affair with Maria has troubled me. He has never explained himself. I didn't know of Gonzalez. That is a serious black mark against him."

"Then I have your promise you will not see him nor speak of him further?"

Leinani nodded.

He left.

Gunter rose from his seat when Grant entered his Honolulu office. "Well, you made good time from Wailuku. Follow me."

They entered the inner chamber of the business suite. Grant directed his underling to a chair before his highly polished desk that shone like burnished gold. As was his custom he reached for his humidor, selected a cigar, placed it to his ear and squeezed, heard the leafy crackle and snipped an end, lit up, and blew smoke.

He thought about his visit with his daughter. Her charity made him strangely happy. "At least there is one good thing I have done in my life," he muttered.

Gunter shifted in his seat and drew closer to the desk. "What did you say."

"Nothing of importance. I'm sure you're wondering why I asked you here."

Gunter nodded.

"You recall that scalawag, John Tana."

"Can't forget him."

Grant withdrew the Colt and box of ammunition. "I want you to polish him off. He's due back from Molokai soon. He'll be an easy target for you at the harbor."

"I don't understand why you want to do this. You know the last time I tried he broke my arm, it still hurts! And I told you he said, 'He can have my Kahalui land. If he tries to kill me again I will kill him'."

"I know that, but the man is still bothering my family."

"Sir, I have fought this man two times. Twice I have lost. The last time he could have killed me but didn't. Instead, he spared my life and sent me to give you a message. I think you should heed his warning."

"You're afraid of him."

Gunter shifted in his seat, stared at the ceiling, and returned his gaze to his employer. "I am not afraid. But what you want me to do is gun down a local hero who has done nothing to me. I have taken your money in the past, but this time I draw the line. Give up your vendetta against this man before he kills you."

"There is not enough money I can offer you to do the job?"

"An emphatic, no!"

Grant contemplated his options. He would find another way. He put the gun and ammunition back in its drawer, slammed it shut, and said, "You're fired."

Chapter 49

After the steamer had pulled into Honolulu Harbor and goods and horses offloaded, Liliuokalani came to John. "I have been speaking with one of my retainers. He has told me of your splendid detective work. You have won over the haole business community. They want to install you as chief of plantation security on this island. Congratulations! I'm sure my brother would want to entertain you and give you a reward. Never has a pure Hawaiian achieved the status you have gained."

John smiled. "I have thought about what you have just said for some time. But there is an old proverb: fame is fleeting. I am returning to Kauai, where I have a good life and can control my fate. To remain here would be a disaster. Our captain, once reloaded, is heading to my home. I am going with him."

"That is sad. I'm sure we could find an important office for you to hold in our government."

"The only position I would consider would be head of the Hawaiian militia. But your brother says no. Someday the kingdom will be sorry it does not have an armed force to protect it. Instead of trips around the world and building an expensive palace money is better spent on military preparedness."

"I fear if we become more military American businessmen will pursue annexation more forcefully. It is a dangerous time for the kingdom. My brother's trip around the world has proved less advantageous than he thought. There are complaints about his spending on that venture, and his decision to build a palace mirroring the French Versailles has angered many."

"I know nothing of politics like you, but I have heard stories of the great Kamehameha from my grandfather. He united these islands. He was a warrior king, a man unafraid. He understood the need to use force to attain his goal, one kingdom for these islands."

Liliuokalani nodded. "He was a great man. But the missionaries taught us that warfare will not win against the power of the western world. Guns and cannon are better than sharp sticks and stones. We must appear civilized and not act like savages making threats. Look at this harbor with its British, French, and American warships. It is a tinderbox, at any time it could explode and one nation land troops to seize our kingdom. It's only their rivalry, their fear that one nation would take this jewel in the Pacific for themselves, that keeps us independent."

With a sigh, John answered, "In my life, I have been forced to use my lua training, my physical skills to overcome those who would destroy me. What you say is that personal strength cannot deal with this new world that has been forced on these islands by Captain Cook. I wish he had never come. All he brought is disease, leprosy, and alcohol. This is what is destroying our people."

"What you say is true. We are a vanishing race. That is the reason my brother said on his inauguration: 'We must end the process of decay and increase our people.' That is a goal which I believe will save our nation."

"You will not accomplish your aim as long as whites are in control."

"Let us not talk any more on that subject, although I will say that my brother will be appointing Walter Gibson as Premier of Hawaii. He is pro-Hawaiian."

"Before we part, may I ask a favor of you? Could one of your retainers deliver this letter to James Kingsley? I am declining any offer of a job on Oahu and returning permanently to Kauai."

"I will do as you ask. Farewell, John Tana. The kingdom owes you much. My brother and I are grateful for all you have done."

Chapter 50

Grant stared at his cards. Two Kings, three would be better, he thought, but in five hand poker it is not bad. He glanced at his companions. Donald Cartwright's face was impassive, his eyes studiously fixed on the table, giving nothing away. Next to him, Bruce Jones puffed on his cigar spewing smoke copiously into the room. Nervous, uncertain, Grant thought. The fourth man, Allen Tucker, had laid his cards down, conceding his involvement in the game.

"You seem to be studying the green felt very closely, Donald. Is anything wrong?"

"Not in the least. I'm just contemplating, Robert, how easy it will be to take your money."

"Stop baiting each other. Whose turn is it to bet?" Jones asked. Smoke billowed from his lips.

"It must be mine. With what I have I'll throw in fifteen," Grant said.

Cartwright's face wreathed into a smile. "I think you're bluffing. I'll match and raise you twenty."

Jones gasped, "Thirty-five to me!" He stared at his cards, stubbing out his cigar in an ashtray nearby. He waved a hand as if clearing smoke from his eyes. He looked at the stakes on the table, a sizable pot. He stared at his companions. With a flourish, he fanned his cards down. "I'm out."

Grant folded his cards, and then spread them open. He looked at Cartwright who was again staring at the green felt of the poker table. What did he have? Were two royals enough to beat him? On the table lay the biggest stakes of the game, over a hundred dollars. He brought his cards together again, laid them on the table, and reached for a humidor.

"Beaten?"

"Nonsense, just enjoying a cigar while I contemplate how much to raise." He shrewdly looked at Cartwright. Did his hand shake?

He took his time, testing the tightness of the wrap of the weed, smelling its aroma, lighting the stogie. He watched his opponent and saw trembling. He had bullied people before and knew the effects of his bluster. "Call and raise you thirty."

There came a pause as players looked at Cartwright who contemplated his cards. Tension built.

At that moment James Kingsley entered the private chambers of the Downtown Club.

"Aha, you are finally here," Grant said. "Gentlemen, this is a friendly game. We played cards while we waited for my son-law. We have more important things to discuss than determining a winner or loser. Best we attend to business. I propose a draw."

"I think he is bluffing. Call him," Tucker said.

Without hesitating Cartwright said, "This is a friendly game. It could turn ugly on a turn of the cards. I accept a draw. None of our cards will be revealed."

"Done. Gentlemen I brought you here to discuss a very disturbing problem. While I tended to business on Maui a kanaka has fooled this community by being allowed to make himself into a folk hero. I can tell you the many evil things about this man, but suffice it to say that we cannot exalt a Hawaiian to a position of respectability in Honolulu. Natives have never owned a plantation, or merchandising business, or any enterprise of value. Only Anglo-Saxons, the fine people of English heritage, have accomplished these achievements. We have been the salvation of this economy and we must not waste all the good we have done by giving a native some form of undeserved reward."

"You echo my thoughts," Cartwright said. "I know when Tucker first approached me on the subject of a security job for this person, I had great reservations. Look at our king, all he knows to do is spend money, drink, and have sex parties. This man could be of the same ilk. Isn't he a friend of Kalakaua?"

"Yes," Jones answered. "Listen to me. The problem is greater than you men realize. The king plans to appoint Walter Murray Gibson as Premier of the nation. He will be a disaster for us. All his speeches in the legislature have been trumpeting 'Hawaii for Hawaiians'. We cannot give any native the appearance of being a success in this society."

"I'm sorry to hear what is being said. The man saved June and me from death. I hold nothing against him. But I understand your desire for white supremacy in this nation," Tucker said.

"Gentlemen, if your concern is about offering this man a security job in Honolulu, your worries are over. I have received a letter from John Tana advising that he declines our offer and is returning to his home in Koolau. Unless my father-in-law wishes to pursue some form of criminal charges against him, I suggest we let him go."

"Jim, thank you for this information, I agree we should let him go. We have more serious problems to deal with. Sometime in the future I will find a way to deal with the wrongs this man has inflicted upon me. Gentlemen, let's play cards. This time there will be no draws."

Chapter 51

Kauai

His transport went no further than Kapaa. There, John secured a horse and rode north. *As he traveled he thought of all the things he had learned in the big city. Most troubling of all is what Still had said. Could the fear of leprosy be used as an excuse to eradicate Hawaiians? From what he had observed at the leper colony, it appeared to be the objective of the Health Department.*

It was a foreigner, a Belgian priest who had helped bring order out of the horrible conditions that existed on that isolated peninsula. *For some reason, the Hawaiian kings had not protected their people from the horror. Why had they failed? As he rode he prayed that Liliuokalani could convince her brother to stem the misery of his people.*

The news of his return to Koolau had preceded him. People stood along the roadway waving him onward. Many presented him lei as he traveled. By the time he reached home, there were eager families awaiting him, all seeking information about loved ones, lepers incarcerated in the colonies of Kalawao and Kalaupapa.

His family had prepared a feast. There was food for everyone, another reminder that in Hawaiian families, when matters of the heart are involved, there is no guest list.

He embraced Mahelani who had tears in her eyes when he held her. "I've missed you and the children."

"I missed you, too."

Before they could say more the couple was thronged by anxious people wishing to learn about loved ones. John spent his time answering as many questions as he could.

After the feast, a feeling of well-being hung over the room. There was much aloha expressed for each other. When John rose to speak, there came a respectful hush. He began with stories he had heard at the restaurant days before. He spoke of the terror faced by the lepers as they were prodded into the sea. His words were often interrupted by labored breathing and stifled sobs. Tears flowed as he described the bleakness of the peninsula, the loneliness, and sad condition of the inmates. He described their falling fingers and toes, the odors, and so many other horrors faced by men, women, and children who had done nothing more than become ill.

John received wide applause when he told of the kokua and their unselfish work. He described how the princess visited Kalawao and wept when the leper choirs sang. The images he painted were so vivid that many of his listeners cried in happiness. John ended his talk with words of encouragement, reminding the group that Father Damien was inspirational, that Princess Liliuokalani had vowed to spend more money and make things better for the people imprisoned in the colony.

When John concluded, Al Akaka embraced him. "What you said is important for these to hear. Molokai is not the best place for our people. Did you see any white lepers there?"

"No."

"Then what you said about it being a graveyard for Hawaiians is true. Only the poor commoners are sent there."

"There are Chinese among the Hawaiian lepers."

"This is tokenism, a smokescreen for the true intentions of those in control. There are some on this island who are rebelling against the harsh policies of our government."

"What kind of rebellion?"

"They're refusing to go to Kalawao. Many of them have fled with their families to Kalalau Valley."

"This is wise. That valley in the mountains on the northwest side of the island is reachable only by boat during the summer and at other times by difficult trails over the mountains. It is an ideal place to hide from the sheriff. Is there a leader of the lepers?"

"I think you know of him, Judge Kauai and his wife, Kaenaku."

"*Auwe*, a good man, I supported his election to the legislature. People in Waimea love him. He has the skill and leadership, to make that small community of lepers thrive."

"We are sending what is needed," a woman overhearing the conversation revealed. "These poor people deserve to live and die with dignity."

A short and very round man standing at her side placed a hand on the woman's shoulder. He looked at John and asked, "Are you aware that many members of the Caucasian community are supporting this rebellion?"

"No."

"There have been police who have tried to make arrests of lepers in Waimea. They have been met with dozens of men with guns. Some of them are foreigners. These people have helped the sick to escape to Kalalau."

When the crowd had thinned John finally had time be alone with Mahealani. "Tell me about the children."

"Your son JJ managed to mix chicken manure in our daughter's beauty cream, so you can imagine her response."

John laughed, shaking his head at his son's behavior. "And he managed to avoid Nani's revenge?"

Mahealani rolled her eyes, but it was clear that she felt more concern than enjoyment. "All was calm…until yesterday. I thought Nani had finally given up chasing him, but I was wrong. Our son returned home from school hungry and in tears because tadpoles were swimming in his poi lunch. You must make peace between them. Revenge must stop."

John winced at the word *revenge*. He took his wife's hands in his own, and searched her eyes, surprised to find them no longer clouded with fear. She had grown, as had he in the time that he had been away.

John reached into his pocket and retrieved the locket. He opened Mahealani's hand and placed it into her palm. "A holy man, Father Damien, gave this to me. It's for you. There's a healing prayer inside."

He opened the locket. "Before I left Kalawao, he blessed our family, and promised to pray for Edward, asking God to give him eternal peace."

Mahealani turned the heart-shaped gift in her hand, saw the face of a young mother, a child in her arms, etched into the porcelain. The woman seemed to be smiling and this caused Mahealani to smile as well. "Please," she asked, handing the locket to John.

He took the chain and fastened it around her neck. With the lovely image of the Virgin Mary lying on her bosom, Mahealani reached up and said, "I love you."

Hand in hand, they walked outside and sat on the veranda of their new home. The air was cool and a deep blue glow filled the sky. A light evening breeze carried with it the sounds of lowing cattle and fussing hens. At a house nearby, Moana strummed his guitar, a young woman's voice sang a Hawaiian song. Mahealani drew John into her. "I am happy," she said, mixing her breath with his. "We have a beautiful home, a good school for the children, and a farm."

John stroked Mahealani's hair and smiled, "Yes, security work has been good for us. Despite my earlier anger, I am forced to be grateful to the sugar plantations. I hope our happiness will last forever."

A full moon was just becoming visible above the horizon, casting a silvery shimmer across the water and into the veranda. In the stillness of the early night, a woman's voice sang:

Birds of the forest sing a sweet song.
Blossoming gardenias fragrant the air.
The night is filled with your beauty.
You are the one that I love and adore.
You are the choice of my heart forevermore.

Mahealani snuggled into John. He pulled her close until her body melded with his. They listened to the love song as the moon shone silver on the vast and beautiful land of John and Mahealani Tana.

About the Author

Bill Fernandez, half-native Hawaiian, was born and raised on the small island of Kauai in the Hawaiian Islands. An alumnus of Kamehameha Schools, Stanford University, and Stanford Law School, he practiced law in Sunnyvale, CA, home to the future Silicon Valley, and served on the Sunnyvale City Council and as mayor. Bill served twenty years as judge of the Santa Clara County Courts. Retired, he and his wife, Judith, live on Kauai where he writes and gives author talks. He served as president and member of the board of the Kauai Historical Society, on the board of a social service agency, Hale Opio, and the Native Hawaiian Chamber of Commerce. He is a member of the State of Hawaii Juvenile Justice State Advisory Commission.

Bill and his wife enjoy the ocean breezes sitting on the lanai of the old plantation cottage Bill inherited from his mother. They are avid travelers and opera lovers.

Judge William J. Fernandez, ret.

County of Santa Clara Courts, California
www.kauaibillfernandez.com fcb: Bill Fernandez Hawaiian Author

GLOSSARY

ahupuaa	land division, mountains to the sea	*aikane*	friend
amakua	personal god	*ana ana*	death dealer
awa	potion	*ha*	breath
hui	club, organization	*kahuna*	priest
kanaka	man	*kilu*	Hawaiian sex game
kapa (tapa)	barkcloth made from pounded inner bark of paper mulberry trees	*kokua*	helper
la aula paau	healer	*luna*	supervisor
mai pake	leprosy	*ohana*	family
pake	Chinese	*piikoi*	club weapon
pueo	Hawaiian owl	*uhane*	ghost

Note: Hawaiian words often have diacritical marks such as the okina (looks like an apostrophe) which affects the meaning and pronunciation. For ease of reading by a broad audience, I am not including the okina or other diacritical marks in the Hawaiian words.

Made in the USA
Las Vegas, NV
22 March 2024

87611363R00142